HOW TO
D♥TE A
Younger
MAN

New York Times & *USA Today* Bestselling Author

KENDALL
RYAN

How to Date a Younger Man

Copyright © 2020 Kendall Ryan

Developmental Editing by Rachel Brookes
Copy Editing by Pam Berehulke
Cover Design and Formatting by Uplifting Author
Services

ABOUT THE BOOK

Tips for Surviving a Fling with a Sexy Younger Man

First, you'd think as a thirty-something-year-old woman, I'd be immune to Griffin's flirty comments and six-pack abs. You'd think that his carefree playboy attitude, or the fact that he's still finishing grad school, would deter me.

You'd be wrong.

If you accidentally bang your best friend's younger brother, here are a few important tips . . .

One: Do *not* brag to your friend about how well-endowed her brother is.

Two: Do not go back for seconds (or thirds).

Three: Do not let him see your muffin top or jiggly behind. And definitely don't let him feed you cookies in bed. Cookies are bad. Remember that.

Four: Act like a damn grown-up and apologize for riding him like a bull at the rodeo. And *do not* flirt with him when he laughs at said apology.

Five: This one is crucial, so pay attention.

Do *not*, under any circumstances, fall in love with him.

ONE

Griffin

Four years ago

"Here goes nothing," I mutter to myself.

After double-checking the address one last time, I haul the massage table through the wide front doors of the chrome-and-glass building downtown. Anderson and Associates is a lucrative law firm and as I ride the elevator up to the fifteenth floor, I pray to God that I'm not going to be rubbing down some wart-covered, age-spotted, pasty old bastard for the next ninety minutes.

I shudder at the thought. It wouldn't be the first time though because it kind of comes with the territory of being a massage therapist. You just never know who you're going to meet.

I finished my undergrad degree in business last year, but since I have no idea what I want to do with my life, I decided to take a year off to figure out my path. And since I still needed to make money, I'd gotten a massage therapist license. I've always been good at talking to people, making them comfortable and feeling at ease. I guess working with my hands is just an extension of that talent.

But it's certainly not my forever. I'm set to start grad school in the fall and I'll be studying architecture, which will be quite a departure from rubbing elderly people down with lavender-scented oil daily. But, whatever, the money's been good and has lessened the stress of my finances.

I stop in front of a desk inside the office and feel the young receptionist's appreciative gaze drift over my broad shoulders and muscular pecs visible under my black T-shirt.

"Hi. I'm here for an appointment with . . ." I glance down at the details on my phone. "Mr. Layne Anderson."

"Miss Anderson," the receptionist says, correcting me. "And yes, right this way. We've been expecting you."

She rises to her feet and escorts me down the hall toward a corner office. Inside, a woman with long dark hair sits behind a huge glass-topped desk, her gaze glued to the screen of her laptop and her fingers flying over the keyboard.

The receptionist knocks on the door frame. "Layne?"

The woman looks up, and her gaze lands on mine.

A pulse of excitement flickers through me. *Damn, she's sexy as hell.* Not very professional, I know, but it's the first thought that pops into my head. I'd expected a man because of her name— Layne, pronounced as Lane.

I guess there's a reason MILF porn is the most popular search on the internet. And my client this afternoon? She's the living, breathing proof of why those fantasies exist. She's polished and poised. Exquisitely beautiful and sure of herself in a way that most twenty-somethings aren't. Myself included.

"Can I help you?" she asks, quickly appraising me before sending a curious glance to her assistant.

I wish I could say that I'm straining to imagine what the shape of her body is under that white button-up shirt and tight gray skirt for professional reasons. Usually, a quick assessment is needed— how is their posture, are there any visible signs of tension in the shoulders and neck, et cetera. But with the woman's inquisitive gaze on me, I've forgotten my own damn name, let alone why I'm standing in her office.

"Happy birthday, boss." The receptionist smiles, patting me on the shoulder.

We're still standing in the doorway of the office, so I take a small step forward, holding up the folded massage table with a half smile.

The woman's brow furrows in confusion. *She has no idea what's happening.*

Inwardly, I grimace. Office massages are sometimes given as gifts between coworkers, but my services have never been a surprise gift before. Because . . . you know, it's intimate.

Wow. Her assistant has some serious balls.

"Thank you." She smiles diplomatically and stands up, striding over to us with a sharp click of her heels.

When she outstretches a hand to me, a fantasy of those small, slender hands whispering over my forearms and biceps almost overwhelms me. But her hand slides into mine and doesn't wander any further.

"Layne Anderson," she says with a curve of her

full red lips.

"Griffin." I grasp her hand, noting her handshake is firm and strong. A little bolt of electricity zips through me at the contact and I wonder if she felt it too.

"I'll leave you to it, then," the receptionist says. "I'll forward your calls to voice mail for the next hour, okay?" She moves around the room, closing all the blinds, effectively blocking us off from the eyes of any curious coworkers.

"Wait. I appreciate this, I truly do," Layne says, her palms up and open. "But I don't have the time."

So she's gathered why I'm here. Thank God. Explaining would have been a first. "Hello, ma'am, it's time for you to get naked from the waist up and let me stroke you with scented oils. Am I moving too fast?"

"But, Layne—"

"How much did you pay for this, anyway?" Layne plants her hands firmly on her hips.

I would be annoyed—being referred to as *this*—but I'm too aware of the fact that I'm about to be dismissed. And that can't happen for two reasons.

"I'm afraid I'm nonrefundable," I say, flashing

my best *I'm totally harmless* smile. I can't tell if it's working on this woman, though.

Layne's gaze flicks to me and then back to her employee. She's making a decision. I hope it's the right one, because something inside me isn't ready to go.

"Sorry. Just make the most of it," the receptionist whispers with exaggerated subservience, and then ducks out of the room.

Their dynamic is fascinating, to say the least. Layne's employees love her enough to gift her a three-hundred-dollar massage, but they clearly don't know her very well. I'm still not sure she's completely on board with this. Luckily, I have no problem getting up close and personal.

The door clicks shut, leaving the two of us alone inside the spacious office, and I swallow, fighting a suddenly dry mouth.

She sighs, almost begrudgingly. "I suppose you won't let me just fake this whole thing? Lie to my employees and tell them you gave me a life-changing massage?" she asks with a tilt of her head.

Her hair drops over one shoulder, and I find myself thinking, yet again, with the wrong organ.

"It's entirely up to you," I say, mirroring her

body language in an attempt to make her more comfortable. "I have to say, though, a massage never hurt anyone."

"Tell that to my in-box," she says with a smirk. With one final, searing look, she turns her back on me and removes her blazer.

I guess we're doing this.

"Is there something I need to change into?" she asks, eyeing the small duffel bag slung over my shoulder.

"I'll put the table together first. It'll only take five minutes. Then I can either step out while you remove your clothing above the waist and lie down on the table under the sheet, or you can change in the restroom while I handle the minor assembly, and then come out when you're ready."

I'm impressed with how professional I sound right now, even though the tingling sensation in my stomach is undoubtedly on a surefire journey toward my groin. If I get a hard-on on the job, I'm going to fire myself.

"Whatever will get this over with sooner," she grumbles. It's actually adorable how reluctant she is to be pampered.

Adorable? What's wrong with me? I should be

hella annoyed that this lady is being so difficult. I make the conscious decision to meet her lack of enthusiasm with an equal lack thereof.

"You do you," I say with a rehearsed shrug and my most flirtatious smirk.

She squints at me in the way my parents did when I first uttered the words *that's what she said* in their presence. It's a mix of confusion with a hint of disbelief.

Way to make yourself look like a douche, man.

Before I can follow up with something, *any-thing*, to make up for it, she retreats through a door connecting to a private restroom. Before she closes it behind her, she peeks her head out.

"Five minutes?" she asks, and when I nod, she closes the door behind her.

Damn. I wish I lived a life in which my work-place provided a personal adjoining bathroom to my office. My office is this table, which I yank this way and that until it follows my orders.

Needing something to place my accessories on, I scan the room and spot a small coffee table that will work perfectly. I drag it over to the massage table and unpack my lotions, oils, and portable speaker. I scroll through my phone, select my favorite Chill Vibes playlist, and set the volume on low. The soft music plays pleasantly in the background and in just a few minutes I'm ready for her.

It occurs to me that five minutes was plenty of time for her to undress . . . too much, even. I wonder if she's standing on the other side of the door, topless and waiting.

My dick twitches in my pants. I take a deep breath, drip some lavender oil on my wrists, and inhale again. I need to calm down if I'm going to do my job well.

The door cracks open a sliver, and she asks, "Are you ready for me?"

My dick full-on throbs at that question. *Jesus Christ.*

"Yes, I'm facing the far wall. Come lay face down on the table."

"Yes, sir."

I can hear her sexy little chuckle from across the room. Focusing on the world outside her window, I desperately try not to seek out the reflection of her naked torso in the glass. *Don't be a fucking pervert, Griff.*

"Ready."

I didn't even hear her get on the table. She must have taken off her heels. I turn around to find them coupled perfectly by her desk.

Even more perfect is her half-naked body laying on my table. I take a quick moment to take in the sheet bunched up around her hips, the softness of her bare back, and her hair pulled neatly to one side. Layne is wildly outside of my frame of reference and if I'm being honest, she's completely out of my league.

I approach her naked back like I'm Indiana Jones, and any wrong move could result in flying spears and huge boulders hurtling toward me. But the closer I get, the less nervous I become. I find myself fascinated by the curve of her spine, the little freckles on her shoulders that speckle her otherwise blemish-free skin.

"Can I use oil?" I ask, my voice husky and low.

It's a standard customer-service question in this line of work, but I feel as awkward as if I'd just asked her if I could finger her. I watch as the fine, pale hairs that trail the length of her back stand up in arousal. *Holy shit.*

"Yes, please," she says with a sigh.

She's finally giving in.

I pour a little lavender oil into my hands and rub them together to create a warm friction.

When my fingers make contact with her back, my mind goes completely blank. I don't know what comes over me, but I know for a fact that I'm about to give this gorgeous woman the best massage I've ever given.

And this time, it's not about customer service at all.

TWO

Layne

It's a quarter to two on a Tuesday afternoon, and for the first time in over a decade, I'm not thinking about my next three cases. I'm not thinking about how to negotiate with a pushy board of directors, or when I can find the time to shove a quick protein-bar down my throat for dinner.

All of the above are far from my realm of thought right now because the only thing on my mind is the twenty-something piece of man candy working his strong, determined hands over my tight, knotted shoulders. And, trust me, there is not one single thing I hate about it.

Ever since I took the leap and opened my own law firm, the team of corporate-law badasses I employ have stuck to pretty generic boss gifts for my birthday. A nice box of chocolates, a case of wine from a local vineyard, or a gift basket filled with artisan crackers and smelly cheeses.

But this year, they apparently decided to think outside the box. And by outside the box, I mean they sent a hottie probably young enough to be my son into the office to rub lavender-scented oil all over my body for the next ninety minutes. As if I didn't already know they all secretly thought I was an uptight workaholic, now they were hoping to have it rubbed out of me.

I'd be lying if I said my birthday present isn't delivering. I can't imagine that he grew up wanting to massage strangers' bodies for a living, but the way he's unraveling the knots along my shoulder blades, you'd think it was his God-given calling.

"How's the pressure? Am I pressing too hard?"

His low, soothing voice barely registers with me, and I simply purr a soft "it's perfect" in response. He's been attentive and careful from the moment his hands came into contact with my skin, and it's only made me more relaxed. In fact, I haven't felt this relaxed in a long time. It's making me consider adding regular massages into my already jam-packed schedule. I'd definitely find the time if it meant feeling like this.

After massaging my shoulders and neck so well I'm practically drooling and lucid, his hands leave my body for good and I miss the feeling of his fingers immediately.

"Take a few minutes to come back to earth, and make sure you drink plenty of water for the rest of the day," he says, stepping away from the table. He wanders over to one of the floor-to-ceiling windows I fought tooth and nail for, overlooking the bustling city below.

"I'm not sure I'm ready to come back yet," I murmur, only half-aware that I'm thinking out loud.

He chuckles, and the sound is deep and rich. "It's fine. Take your time."

I blink open my eyes and see him standing across the room, facing the windows and looking out into the world. He looks comfortable—relaxed even—in my impeccably arranged corner office, which is rare for anyone under the age of thirty. I've had a handful of tech kid geniuses in here looking for legal counsel before selling their apps, and they never seem to know what to do with themselves, bouncing around with nervous energy, or sweating through their ill-fitting button-downs. I don't know if this kid works in the corporate world often, but it's clear he's not intimidated by a woman in power and I've got to admit, I like that. A lot.

"That was exactly what I needed. Thank you," I reply, slowly pulling myself together.

The awareness that I'm half naked under this thin white sheet seems to knock some sense into me. Carefully turning over while still keeping myself covered, I swing my legs over the side of the table, holding the sheet up over my chest.

He doesn't turn around, and I take the opportunity to admire the muscles that fill out his fitted black shirt. Ten years ago, he would have been exactly the kind of guy who would get me in a lot of trouble. The kind of guy you assume wants the same things you do, until you wake up six months later and find yourself wondering why he hasn't introduced you to his friends yet.

I shake my head, grateful to be past all that twenty-something bullshit. It didn't come easy, but I can confidently say I feel perfectly complete without a man. I've been focused on myself and my career for the past decade, and I'm genuinely proud of where I'm at. But that doesn't mean I want to be alone forever. It would be nice to have a partner to share this crazy, fast-paced life with, but I haven't found the right guy yet.

"Be right back," I say, heading into the private

restroom connected to my office.

Once inside, I crumple the sheet and set it on the counter. I quickly slip back into my nude-colored bra, crisp white button-down shirt, and gray tweed pencil skirt. Then I take stock of myself in the mirror, fluffing up my flattened hair and wiping away the smudge of mascara from beneath my right eye.

I take a step back and give myself a once-over.

My shiny dark hair is threaded with golden strands, thanks to regular appointments with my colorist, and my cheeks have a healthy glow. My breasts, while full, aren't exactly where they're supposed to be. Gravity has shifted them a couple of inches lower than I would prefer. But I'm relatively fit and take good care of my skin. Thank God for SPF. It's something, I guess. But even as I look myself over, I noticed that my features look more relaxed than usual. I smile. Maybe Griffin was good for me.

When I step into my office again, Griffin is exactly where I left him.

He turns, a confident smirk pulling at the corner of his mouth. "I'll bet you have a great view of the sunset from here."

"Unbelievable, actually." I wander closer to

where he's standing.

He turns to meet my eyes. "I know a spot with an even better view. How about I take you there sometime?"

Wait. What?

Did this infant just ask me out?

My stomach does a backflip, and for a second, I'm flattered. But the reality of the situation hits me quickly—and hard.

Is he even legal drinking age? Regardless, he's clearly several years younger than me. If this kid would have been my kryptonite in my twenties, now, in my thirties? He's jailbait. I don't know what kind of mommy issues he's looking to work out, but I don't have time for any of that bizarre Freudian stuff.

"Oh, uh, you're kind, and it's very sweet of you to offer, but that's not necessary," I say, uncharacteristically stumbling over my words.

He blinks, and then an amused smile overtakes his face. "Are you single?"

I clear my throat and then lick my lips, which have suddenly gone dry. Maybe that water he suggested is a good idea. "Well . . . yes, but I don't see what that has to do with anything."

He takes a step closer and I suck in a desperate breath and wait for whatever this weird feeling in my stomach is to fade. "Come on, you can't tell me that you're so out of practice that you can't tell when a man is asking you out." There's a hint of a smile on his full lips.

I stay quiet. This is absolutely none of his business.

"You're gorgeous," he says, his voice dropping low, "and you're obviously very successful. I think we could have some fun. Unless you're not attracted to me? Is that it?"

Ha! The most devout nun on the planet would be attracted to him. But he's not my type. I'm looking for someone stable, someone my own age, someone ready for marriage and babies, sooner rather than later. These eggs of mine have an expiration date, a little fact I'm acutely aware of, unfortunately.

"I'm flattered, honestly, but I'm too busy, and too old for a fling with my company birthday present."

"You sure about that?" he asks, his lips still tilted in a smile.

I nod. "I'm very sure."

His gaze lingers on my lips as I speak, and my stomach does this weird twisting thing again. And, wow, he smells good. Like fresh laundry and lavender and man.

Since I'm not sure what else to say, I go with the obvious. "You do realize I'm a lawyer, right? Aren't we supposed to maintain some level of professionalism here?"

"Based on what I've seen in this building, you do corporate law. So, unless you're about to facilitate the acquisition of the company that pays my rent, I think we're good here."

I chuckle, taken aback by his awareness of what I do. Something tells me there's more to him than meets the eye. But that doesn't mean I'm about to stick around to find out what.

As I watch, he efficiently folds up the table and gathers the discarded sheets.

"If you change your mind, you know where to find me." He shoots me one last smile, setting his card on my desk before walking out of my office, and lets the frosted glass door shut behind him.

What the hell just happened?

Pushing my fingers through my hair, I sit back down at my desk and desperately try to remember what I'm supposed to be doing. But, honestly? I'm having a little trouble focusing.

Do women in their mid-thirties really get asked out by twenty-something hunks in tight black T-shirts? The longer I try to push it out of my mind, the more the whole thing seems like a weird dream—or a bad porno with me being the lead actress.

But before I can imagine how that particular scenario might play out, my phone beeps once and Sabrina speaks over the intercom.

"Layne, I have Susanna from Fir Industries on line two for you."

Taking a deep breath, I roll my shoulders and center myself. I need to get back in the zone. I'm a lawyer—a damn good one—and I refuse to let a sexy as hell distraction distract me from what I do best.

"Thanks, Sabrina. I'm ready, you can connect me."

The rest of the day goes by in a blur of conference calls and contract negotiations, but I'd be lying if I said my thoughts didn't keep wandering back to that massage. Every time I move my arm to pick up the phone, I get a waft of the lavender-scented body oil he so expertly used, sending me right back to that table.

As I'm packing up my things, Sabrina pokes her head in my doorway, a nosy, sheepish smile on her face.

"So . . . how did it go?"

"The contract is almost finalized. We just have a few more tweaks to make in the morning."

"We both know I'm not referring to the contract. The hot masseur, how did that go? I've heard rumors about the kind of hunks they employ over there, but wow, your guy was something else."

I blink trying to find the right thing to say without giving too much away. "He was . . . young."

"Oh, come on. Don't tell me there wasn't some part of you that wanted to take him home and show him who's boss."

I pause to arch a brow at her.

"With his consent, of course," she adds quickly.

"Glad to see all that HR training is really taking root."

She shrugs and crosses her arms. "I know you're this high-powered businesswoman, and don't get me wrong, I'm the first to support you being all ethical about how you use your power."

"Sabrina . . ."

"But you're still allowed to have some fun, you know."

I don't respond, instead giving her a knowing look and slinging the strap of my leather tote over my shoulder. "Good night, Sabrina. I'll see you at the meeting tomorrow morning."

"Goodnight, Layne."

As I walk through the parking lot toward my car, I can't ignore the nagging feeling that Sabrina has a point. It doesn't matter if the massage thera-pist is young, or less than settling-down material. He was freaking hot, and surprisingly smart and kind. Plus, he asked me out, which meant he was into me too.

But just because Mr. Hottie Pants has a secret MILF fantasy doesn't mean I'm going to abandon my master plan. I know exactly what I'm looking for, and he definitely isn't it.

THREE

Layne

Once I've pressed SEND on my last email of the day, I check the clock in the bottom corner of my screen. It's a few minutes after five already.

Shit. I'm going to be late.

After quickly packing my things into my black leather tote bag, I check my reflection in the dark computer screen before leaving. I mastered my everyday lawyer-lady makeup look years ago—a clean, classic, no-fuss eye paired with a natural rosy lip. But lately, I've been wondering how well it transitions to the Friday night happy-hour scene.

I fish a slightly deeper red lipstick out of my bag and tap some onto my lips, blending the pigment with my finger. It doesn't make a huge difference, but at least it'll look like I put a little effort into my look.

It's not until I'm sitting in my car, on my way to meet my friend Kristen for happy hour, that I breathe a sigh of relief. It's Friday, and I'm sure as hell glad this week is over. Not that it was any crazier than any other week, I'm just thankful for a couple of days to sleep in and regroup. Although, if I'm honest with myself, there's no way I won't spend at least three hours a day this weekend catching up on paperwork.

Mostly, I'm excited to see Kristen. We met several years ago at a spin class and instantly hit it off. As a couple of single girls in their twenties trying to make it in Los Angeles, we instantly bonded over the horrors of the LA dating scene and the struggle of trying to fulfill our dreams in this town.

I wouldn't have made it through my twenties without her, but once I quit my big fancy corporate job and opened my own firm, it became increasingly difficult for us to find the time to get together. To make matters even trickier, just as my schedule began to even itself out, she started a new job as a consultant for a handful of boutique firms downtown, helping them keep up with new trends while still maintaining their faithful clientele. She has an eye for that perfect balance between on trend and classic when it comes to fashion, and has been a godsend as I've worked on building my business wardrobe.

At this point, we haven't seen each other in at least three months, so when she texted me last week to see if I could meet up for happy hour after work today, I jumped at the opportunity. We agreed to meet at our regular spot, a cute, low-lit bar a few blocks from my building where we used to down tequila shots and dance the night away in our twenties. Now in our thirties, we discovered it has a killer happy hour, complete with half-off cocktails and free bowls of popcorn.

By the time I walk through the door, I glance at my phone to check my timing. Five thirty. Lucky for me, Kristen knows my workaholic tendencies, so she won't be surprised when I show up fifteen minutes late.

I scan the high-top wooden tables, quickly spotting Kristen's signature auburn curls. She's tucked them loosely behind her temples with gold bobby pins, coordinating with the small gold hoops hanging from her ears. As always, she looks on trend without being too trendy, her straight-legged light-wash jeans perfectly accentuating her waist, with a black-and-white striped sweater artfully half-tucked into the waistline. Her green eyes light up when she sees me.

I set my tote bag on the table, leaning it against the wall. "Sorry I'm late," I say, pulling her in for a hug.

"Don't worry about it. I haven't been here long."

She's lying, based on the fact that all that's left in her glass are a few cubes of ice and the remnants of a yummy-looking pale pink cocktail, but I'm grateful she's so patient with me. Something tells me most people wouldn't normally be quite so willing to wait around for a friend they only see a couple of times a year.

"All right, what are we drinking?"

She orders us a round of grapefruit palomas, and we get straight to catching up.

"So, last time we talked, the dating scene was looking pretty grim. How are things looking now? Have you met anyone interesting?" she asks, resting her elbows on the table and scrunching her freckled nose.

My mind immediately goes to the hot massage therapist from the other day. My birthday present. It's like the harder I try to stop thinking about him, the more he seems to keep popping up. I keep replaying his attempt to get me to go out with him, and I can't forget the feeling of my stomach becoming wishy washy every time his penetrating eyes collided with mine.

I'm a thirty-three-year-old woman with everything going for her. You'd think by now, my steamy daydreams would include something more substantial than rippling biceps and the faint outline of washboard abs through a thin cotton T-shirt. I should be weighing a man's date-ability based on his more grown-up qualities, like the size of his 401k or how often he calls his mother and not on my fantasies of how his fingers would feel on other parts of my body

I push all thoughts of the hottie aside, determined to tuck the whole embarrassing scenario away for good because what could honestly come out of it?

"Ugh, I wish I had something good to report," I say with a sigh, staring at my straw as I swirl it in the liquid in my glass.

"I'll bet whatever you have is better than the guy who took me to his 'favorite bar' after dinner. It was a strip club."

"At least he didn't wait until the third date to tell you that he's actually a polygamist and already has two wives."

"You're kidding me. Two wives? On the third

date?" Her tone is filled with outrage.

Sing it, sister.

"Apparently, he wanted to clear his conscience before trying to take me to bed."

"Wait, isn't polygamy illegal?"

"Oh, it gets better. He's not *legally* married to either of them. They took turns officiating their own ceremony as part of a sacred ritual of love and unity."

"That's fucking nuts."

"He had a tiny man bun. I should have known."

"A man bun? Oh, Layne, sweetie, why?"

"I'm thirty-three, Kris! If it's taken me this long to find someone, clearly I need to start casting a wider net."

"Or maybe you just need to throw the net in a different direction."

"Listen, if any part of me were attracted to women, I'd already be married with a couple of kids by now."

We both laugh, and my mind wanders to the man candy again. Something tells me a younger man isn't what Kristen means by a different direction. But for a moment, I consider telling her about the whole ordeal, from the magic of his hands on my skin to the shock of him asking me out afterward. It was certainly the most interesting thing to happen to me in recent history.

But she launches into one of her latest dating horror stories—a guy who not only insisted on ordering the most expensive bottle of wine on the menu, but also expected her to pay for it—and I decide not to tell her. I can't quite decide if the whole thing is flattering or embarrassing, and at this point, I don't want help finding out.

Once she wraps up her story, a waiter comes by to see if we need another round. We've downed two bowls of popcorn by this point, but my stomach is still growling. Something tells me that one more drink will go straight to my head, and I have to drive home after this.

"I'm okay," I say, closing the cocktail menu and glancing at Kristen.

"Me too." She smiles as we hand the menus to the waiter.

He places our check on the table, and I barely beat her in grabbing it first, quickly slipping him my credit card before she can.

"Too slow, once again," I tease.

She clucks her tongue and crosses her arms. "Well, that just means I'll have to pay for takeout at my place. I was thinking Chinese?"

"This is why I love you."

"Do you think you could give me a ride? My car's in the shop, so I had to Uber here."

"Only if you promise we can get at least two orders of spring rolls."

"The things we do for our friends." She sighs like it's some great hardship while I grin at her.

By the time we pull up in front of Kristen's building, we've already placed our order for delivery. She moved into an adorable apartment last year and has spent every waking moment since making it her own. The last time I saw it, she claimed it was still in progress. So now, almost a full year later, I'm excited to see what she's done with the place.

"Welcome, welcome!" she squeals as we walk through the door, instantly greeted by the subtle yet calming scents of eucalyptus and lavender. We hang our purses on the iron coat rack in the corner, the first stop on the grand tour.

"It smells like a freaking spa in here," I say, admiring the seascape artwork she has hanging near the entryway.

"Oh, that's all my baby brother. I bought an aromatherapy machine ages ago but never got around to actually using it. He just graduated from Northwestern and is crashing with me for a few weeks while he looks for his own place."

I follow her into the kitchen, which isn't huge, by any means, but a good size for one person. Copper pots hang from a rack on the wall, giving the space a warm, homey vibe. We then move to the living room, with a plush cream couch and a warm sand-colored rug over the hardwood floors. She's painted the one brick wall the same shade as the couch and strung some cool-looking yarn artwork across it.

The place is perfect for her, both in size and style, and I'm so happy she's finally living where and how she wants. The only thing that doesn't quite fit is the smell. The spa vibe fits with her style, but something about it feels a little . . . off.

"They teach the art of essential oils at Northwestern?"

"Not quite," a male voice answers from around the corner. It's low and calm, and eerily familiar, but I can't place where I've heard it before.

A tall, dark-haired figure steps forward. I was so busy admiring Kristen's artistic eye, I didn't see him when we first walked in.

I turn to apologize for not noticing him sooner, but stop dead in my tracks when I lay eyes on his face. He has greenish-blue eyes, almost turquoise, and brown hair that's close-cropped on the sides and longer on top. But more than anything, it's his body I can't get over—because I've spent the past few days fantasizing about it. Even without the black T-shirt, I'd recognize those biceps anywhere.

It's *him.* the massage therapist. Here. In Kristen's apartment.

Fuck.

"Hi, I'm Griffin," he says, reaching out to shake my hand. "Kristen's brother."

Oh. Are we pretending we don't know each other? Is that what's happening here?

I close my mouth and twist it into a polite smile, returning his handshake and doing my best not to freak out. Suddenly, I'm overjoyed that I didn't tell Kristen about the massage. I don't know what the fuck is going on, but the last thing I was prepared for was to see him again.

"Griff, this is my friend Layne. She's a badass lawyer and very stressed. Maybe you could put that massage experience of yours to good use and give her some pointers on how to unwind."

Fuck, fuck, fuck.

"Hey, we just went to happy hour. Isn't that the definition of unwinding?" I say, praying to whatever god can help me that Griffin doesn't say anything about the fact we've already met. Or that he's already put his hands all over my naked, oily body.

"Happy hour sounds like a start," he says, holding my gaze with a look so intense, my insides immediately flip-flop.

Tearing my gaze away, I look back at Kristen and shrug. "See? I'm wound just fine. Now can we please discuss something more important like how much longer do we have to wait until our food arrives?"

"T-minus . . . five minutes," she replies, checking her phone. "Griff, do you want to join us? As long as you eat like a slightly tipsy thirty-three year-old and not like the twenty-three-year-old frat boy you are, we should have enough lo mein to share."

Twenty-three? Holy fucking shit, he's a baby.

And just like that, I'm happier than ever that I turned him down, and a little embarrassed that I had any kind of tingly thoughts about him since.

He may be legal, but the combination of being a full decade younger than me *and* being Kristen's little brother suddenly makes him even more off-limits. "I'm always down for Chinese," he says, sitting himself smack dab in the middle of the couch and resting both his arms out across the top of the cushions.

"Gee, Griffin, make yourself comfortable. It's not like we have a guest or anything." Kristen rolls her eyes and mouths an apology my way.

I smile and shrug, playing it off like it's not a big deal. And it isn't, really. I'm a lawyer. I play the nonverbal game all the time. He has no idea who he's dealing with.

"What? It's a big couch. If anything, I'm making her more comfortable."

Kristen scoffs. "Clearly."

My mouth turns up into a half smile as I settle into one of the gray armchairs, crossing my legs toward Griffin. He raises his eyebrows, cocking his head at the empty spot next to him in invitation. I only partly meet his gaze in response, tucking my hair behind my ear and turning to Kristen, who's straightening one of the picture frames by her tall wooden bookcase.

"Kris, do you need any help?"

"Nah, I'm fine. Just as anal as ever."

"Since birth, actually." Griffin smirks.

Kristen huffs. "Griff, why don't you make yourself useful and see if our guest wants anything to drink."

He turns his turquoise eyes to me, arching a eyebrow and lifting his chin. "Your wish is my command. Layne, can I be of service and get you something to quench your thirst?"

I roll my eyes. "Water would be great."

"Are you sure you don't want anything stronger? There's plenty of room on this couch if you want to crash here tonight," he says, nodding again to the empty space next to him.

Kristen shoots him a warning glance. "Don't be gross."

"What? I'm being hospitable."

The building intercom buzzes, and my stomach growls happily in response.

"That's the food. I'll run down and get it," Kristen says, grabbing cash out of her purse before leaving the room.

Once the door swings shut behind her, Griffin turns back to me, the look on his face playful and serious at the same time.

"Don't look at me like that," I say, crossing my legs away from him.

"Like what?"

"Like you've seen me naked and had your hands on me."

"But I have seen you naked and I've had my hands on you. Believe me, I could never forget that."

"Not the parts that count."

"I saw enough. Besides, I have a very active imagination."

My stomach lurches. *He's* been imagining *me?* My mind spins a little, thinking about the two of us in different parts of the city, having dirty dreams about each other. Before I can think too hard about any of that, I pull myself together, rolling my eyes and letting out an audible scoff.

"I'm going to get a water," I say, rising to my feet.

Griffin stands up and follows me. In the kitchen, he opens the refrigerator and pulls out a bottle of water to hand to me. "I'm sorry. I'm not trying to make you uncomfortable. The opposite, actually."

As I accept the bottle of water, he rubs his other hand over the back of his neck, looking at me through thick, dark lashes.

"I was trying to pay you a compliment. You're gorgeous, Layne."

I level him with a serious glare, placing one hand on my hip and immediately going on the defense instead of allowing his words to stick because I've never been good at accepting a compliment. "I'm sure you hit on all of Kristen's friends and say all the right things to make them feel special."

He gives me an amused look. "Whatever you have to tell yourself."

"Be serious, Griffin."

Good grief, the guy has six well-defined abs. I have a jiggly ass and a muffin top I have no plans to deal with. A little jiggle never hurt anyone, and I like tacos a hell of a lot more than I like the gym.

"I am being serious. Very serious."

He moves closer to where I'm standing, and I'm trapped—my lower back pressed up against the counter.

Having him so close makes me realize how tall he is. With my heels on, most guys don't tower over me the way Griffin does. And, God, why does he have to smell so good? It's like a mix of cedar and sandalwood and the faintest hint of lavender.

"All I want is a fair chance," he murmurs, his deep voice dropping low.

I swallow a sip of water, trying to regain my composure. "Fine. Tell me about the last date you planned."

This should be entertaining. I don't want to assume but I can't help but think it's going to involve surfing or whatever else young people do in LA. Or maybe he's one of those guys who doesn't believe in dating at all. These days it's all about *Netflix and chill*. . . . whatever that means.

Griffin meets my eyes but takes a second to think about my question. "I had a girl come over and we, uh . . . smoked weed and colored in coloring books." When my eyebrows dart upward, he adds, "They were adult coloring books, if it helps."

I smile unevenly. "It doesn't."

Griffin chuckles at my snarky tone, running one hand through his hair.

"Is that what you would plan to do with me on a date?" I ask.

"No." His tone is firm, and there's a determined crease between his dark eyebrows.

No matter how cute he is, he's got to see this is a terrible idea. Literally, the worst idea ever thought up.

"I'm too old for you," I say, determined and shaking my head. "And I'm your sister's friend. It's never going to happen. It can never happen."

"This is probably a bad time to tell you that I enjoy MILF porn."

"You'd be correct."

"Layne, look. I don't know if you believe in fate or karma or any of that shit—and normally, I don't either. But you and me, coming together like this twice in the same week? I think the cosmic significance is hard to deny."

Cosmic significance? Who the fuck is this guy?

"Your point?"

"My point is, you should let me take you out. At least once. I have a feeling we could have fun together."

I have to hold back a laugh. The last thing I want to do is offend Kristen's little brother. So I chuckle softly, trying to keep the conversation light and almost playful, hoping it might soften the blow.

"I'm serious," he says, his eyes darkening.

My heart sinks a little at the look on his face. I don't want to offend him. But I can tell that I need to be firm and clear with him now, or this will continue to be a problem.

"I know you are, and I think it's sweet. But, really, kid—"

"My name's Griffin."

"Griffin. Look, you seem like a great guy who's very, uh, sure of yourself. But I'm ten years older than you, we are in total different parts of our lives, and you're one of my best friends baby brother."

"Younger brother. There's one more of us who is younger than me, you know."

"Younger brother, fine. My point is, it's never going to happen. I'm done with just dating around for the fun of it. The next relationship I get into is going to be just that—a relationship, full of commitment and plans for the future that includes babies, marriage and everything that comes with finding a forever kind of love. You're twenty-three. You're not ready for forever."

He looks surprised, maybe even stunned, by my response. But before he can counter it, Kristen returns, her arms full of plastic bags, the mouthwatering smell of Chinese food wafting in with her.

"Here, let me help you with that," I say, quickly joining her in the doorway.

She awkwardly hands me a couple of bags, and we take the food to the kitchen, where Griffin still stands near the fridge. He grabs a spring roll and a bottle of water, then disappears back toward the couch without saying a word.

As Kristen and I start plating our food, she leans over to me, raising her eyebrows in the direction of the living room. "Please tell me he hasn't been weird in the two minutes I was gone," she murmurs, a touch of amusement in her voice.

"What? Uh, no, he's been fine," I stammer, taken aback by her comment.

"Ever since he hit puberty, Griffin has been . . . *forward*, to say the least. I'm sorry. If I'd known he was going to be here, I would have warned you."

"Honestly, there's nothing to apologize for. He's totally harmless."

"Okay, well, if he gets gross or comes on to you or anything, don't be afraid to, like, smack him or something."

The image of me smacking his tight ass crosses my mind, but I brush it off. He's Kristen's little brother. And not at all what I'm looking for right now.

"I'll keep that in mind. But, honestly, Kris, it's fine. You have nothing to worry about."

By the time we join Griffin in the living room with food, he's packing up his things to go out and says something about meeting some friends. He doesn't meet my gaze when he says good-bye, but Kristen doesn't seem to notice that anything's up.

She and I spend the rest of the night scarfing down our takeout food and reminiscing about the crazy shenanigans we used to get into in and it makes me feel even more secure in my decision to turn Griffin down.

It might sting for him a little now, but ultimately, it's the right choice for both of us. He has all kinds of fun and trouble to get into in the next few years, and the last thing he needs is to be held back by the expectations of an older woman.

And me? I've got a law firm to run—and a Mr. Forever to find.

FOUR

Griffin

Three years ago

"Griff, are you home?" Kristen calls out as she enters the apartment we share.

"Yeah, in here," I say from where I'm working at the kitchen counter. I've spent the last hour assembling a casserole dish of mushroom-and-spinach lasagna.

"Oh my God, that looks amazing."

She pauses beside me, gazing down into the dish that I've carefully layered with cheese, noodles, and marinara sauce. Cooking isn't something I do regularly so it's obvious she's impressed.

"Mmm, is it vegetarian?" she asks, stealing a sautéed mushroom from the pan and popping it into her mouth.

"Of course." I grin at her, my strange non-meat-eating sister. But, hey, since for the most part, she buys the groceries around here, it would be a major dick move not to accommodate her wishes—even if I miss eating, well, all the dead animals. *God, I'd kill for some bacon.*

"You're my hero. But don't be mad, okay?" She forces a fake smile, narrowing her eyes at me.

I raise a brow in her direction. "Why, what's up?"

"I told Layne we'd meet her at seven at Lario's for appetizers and drinks. She's dating someone new and wants me to meet him."

It's Friday night, and I should have known my sister would want to go out. "I have plans with Wren later anyway. I guess we could join you guys for a drink."

"Awesome. Would you be mad if we popped this in the fridge and had it for dinner tomorrow night? It looks amazing."

I shrug. "That's cool. But because I just spent an hour cooking for you, you're buying my first drink."

Kristen grins. "You have yourself a deal.

Now, go get ready. We leave in thirty." She shoos me away before sauntering into her room. "Yes, ma'am." I quickly finish adding mozzarella cheese to the top, and then cover the whole dish with plastic wrap before placing it in the fridge. Then I grab my phone to text my friend Wren about the change in plans.

Thirty minutes later, Kristen and I stroll into Lairo's, the trendy new bar-restaurant that opened earlier this year in the center of downtown. It's kind of a pain in the ass to get to, but since Layne wants us to meet her new guy, and there's very little I wouldn't do for her … here we are. A large circular bar dominates the center of the room, and several high-top tables are scattered around the perimeter.

I spot Layne right away. She's sitting by herself at one of the high-top tables for six. Rather than staring down at her phone, like anyone else would probably be doing, Layne is people watching. As a lawyer, she has a knack for reading people and I know this because she's always seen straight through all my lines.

But then I notice that her gaze is locked on a couple sitting at the bar. A very touchy couple, from the looks of it. They're turned on their bar stools to face each other, and are holding hands while they talk in hushed tones. A large diamond sparkles on her finger, and he's laughing at something she's said.

When we reach the table, I swear I see a hint of pain in Layne's eyes as she watches the couple interact. It's not exactly a state secret that Layne wants to be settled down in a serious relationship by now. But as quickly as her teary-eyed expression appears, it's gone. She plasters on a smile and rises to her feet to give both Kristen and me a hug.

"Well, where is he?" Kristen asks, her voice filled with excitement.

Layne laughs and motions for us to sit down. "Brian's on his way. He said he was running a little late leaving work tonight."

So he left her sitting here alone? What a jackass. That's a one-point deduction for being a tool, Brian.

A waitress comes by to take our drink orders, and I spot my friend Wren. Rising to my feet so she can see me over the crowd, I give her a quick wave. A happy smile spreads across her face as she heads in our direction.

Wren is a classic case of the ugly duckling. We became friends in grade school, where she was the quirky girl who didn't fit in. I felt bad when I saw her sitting alone at lunch every day, so I started inviting her to eat lunch with me and my group of friends.

Fast forward ten years, and Wren has transformed into a leggy redhead who turns heads wherever we go. My guy friends always want to know why I'm not interested in her, but I've always done my best to keep our friendship purely platonic. Not that I've always been successful. The trouble is, with our complicated past, she can sometimes get jealous when other women take my attention from her. She's basically hated all my girlfriends and isn't afraid to let them know. It's always caused major tension in my relationships, but I value our friendship too much to just stop talking to her.

Wren says hello to Layne and gives my sister a quick hug before taking a seat next to me. "Is this new?" she asks, running a hand over my chest.

I look down, realizing she's referring to the black cashmere sweater I'm wearing. "I don't think so?" I say, wondering if tonight is going to be one of those nights where Wren is going to have a hard time keeping her hands to herself.

When the server comes around, Wren orders a glass of champagne, and another gin and tonic for me. I start to protest, but she puts a hand on my arm.

"It's on me," she says quietly.

She lets her hand linger on my arm for a moment, and I look up to see Layne watching us. I place Wren's hand back in her lap and clear my throat.

Suddenly, I'm not so sure it was a good idea to invite Wren. It's been five minutes, and she's already acting possessive with me. Apparently, I'm the fire hydrant she's trying to piss all over.

"Oh, there he is," Layne says, biting her lip and waving in the direction of the entrance.

Brian's here. *Oh joy.*

Kristen cranes her neck toward the door, and Wren looks bored.

I watch as a guy who looks to be in his late thirties strolls up to the table. His eyes are glued to Layne, and why wouldn't they be? She's still dressed from her day at the office in a formfitting black dress with three-quarter-length sleeves and a knee-length hemline. She looks fucking phenomenal. Her dark hair is secured in a low ponytail, and her wide green eyes sparkle as she watches him approach.

After they share a brief hug, introductions are made around the table. Layne takes the time to give Brian the rundown, covering Wren's business as a party planner, and recounting how she and Kristen met at the yoga studio years ago.

"And this is Griffin, Kristen's younger brother."

Is that really all she sees me as? It takes me a moment to recover, and then I reach one hand out, firmly grasping his in a handshake.

Brian nods, smiling at everyone as he takes the seat next to Layne. "And what do you do, Griffin?"

"I'm studying architecture," I say before polishing off the last of my drink.

"Ah, still in college." He grins conspiratorially at me. "I remember the days."

"Grad school, actually, but yeah, it's great."

A silence falls around us, and Wren leans over to briefly rest her head on my shoulder.

"You okay?" I ask.

She lifts her head, nodding.

"So, Brian, tell everyone about that case you won last week," Layne says, obviously hoping to bring him into the conversation.

He gives her a dismissive wave. "It's not all that interesting a story. My firm found a legal precedent we could use to hold the plaintiff liable."

Brian grabs his beer and takes a swig, and then he rises to his feet. "I need to find the restroom. I'll be back."

When he grasps both of Layne's shoulders and gives them a squeeze as he passes, I have the strange urge to punch the guy for putting his hands on her.

Okay, that's weird. It's not like Layne's never brought a guy around before. There's just something about this one that bugs me.

Maybe it's because I know she thinks it could lead to something serious. And based on the vibe I've gotten in the last five minutes, this guy isn't going to be good enough for her. A smart, gorgeous woman like her deserves someone who's the full package, not some safety-net guy who's going to give her two-point-five kids and a white picket fence while slowly boring her to death.

Once Brian's out of earshot, Kristen flashes Layne a knowing smile. "He seems nice."

Layne nods in agreement. "It's just been so easy with him, you know? No drama, no game playing. It's been great. I finally feel like I found someone I'm on the same page with."

Wren picks at the blood-red polish on her thumbnail.

"What did you think, Griff?" Layne asks, surprising me.

"My opinion matters?" I ask, tipping my glass to my lips and taking a long drink.

A small crease forms between her brows. "Of course it does."

I shrug. "He seems . . ." I search for the right word, narrowing my eyes as I think it over.

Boring. Dull. Like a tool.

Finally, I settle on, "Mature."

Layne's full lips part into a smile, and it eases some of the tension inside me. "Exactly."

As long as she's happy, I should be happy too, right? So, why do I feel angry at the thought of her ending up with a guy like Brian?

Let it go, Griff. It's none of your damn business.

"What did you do last night?" I ask Wren, hoping to move the conversation along to a new topic.

"I broke up with that guy I was dating." Frowning, she takes a sip of her champagne. "He was a snob and terrible in bed. I swear, one more bad date and I'm writing off men. Except you, of course," she says with a smile and a wink for me.

"Sounds like you're better off without him," I say.

"Griffin, sometimes I think you're the only guy who actually knows what a woman needs," she says with a sigh.

"Yeah, and what's that? Someone down to earth who can supply multiple orgasms?" I look right at Layne as the words leave my mouth, and she shakes her head, wearing a knowing smirk.

She sees right through my games, but that's part of our fun.

When Brian returns to the table, our server appears, and we place an order for several appetizers and another round of drinks. And when the perky young waitress turns to saunter away, I watch as Brian's gaze drifts south, lingering on the curve of her ass in her skintight black pants.

Real mature, Brian.

My assumptions were correct. Brian is a tool.

I might not be the right man for Layne, but I'm pretty damn sure that neither is this dick, Brian.

FIVE

Layne

"Cheers, babe, to our six-month anniversary, and to many more to come." I raise my champagne flute and smile at the literal dream-come-true of a man sitting across from me.

Brian smiles back, his chocolate-brown eyes glittering in the warm candlelight of the intimate French restaurant I picked out for our anniversary. My schedule has been packed lately, and it's been a while since we've gone on a real date, so this time, we decided to go all out. After all, it's not every day you get to celebrate spending six months with a man who makes you grateful not to be part of the dating scene anymore.

"Cheers," he replies, clinking his glass to mine.

We're both taking a sip as our server returns with our entrees. Coq au vin for me, and the chef's signature sea bass for him.

My mouth waters at the smell of our food, and watching Brian's face light up brings a smile to mine. This place has been my best-kept secret in the city for five years now, and I'm so happy to finally have someone to share it with.

"*Bon appétit*," the waiter says, bowing slightly.

"*Merci beaucoup,*" I reply.

Brian and I dig in, appreciative moans escaping our lips as we taste the immaculately curated dishes. Each bite is divine, the perfect meal for the perfect anniversary date.

Maybe my stomach doesn't exactly do cartwheels when he's near, but Brian has always made me feel happy and safe. Things with him have just always been so simple.

We met at a law conference, the kind of boring networking event I can barely drag myself out of the office to go to anymore, and from the moment he handed me his business card, I knew Brian was exactly what I was looking for. Mature, successful, attractive. The kind of man you settle down with, who gives you the white picket fence and two-point-five kids. Or in our case, the kind of man who can equally contribute to your mortgage and doesn't bat an eye when you say you need to cancel dinner because a contract is taking longer to pin down than you anticipated.

Although I've thought about our future many times, we haven't actually talked about it yet. I'm hoping that changes tonight. And I'm thinking this might be as good a time as any to finally bring it up and move things in the direction they're naturally heading anyway.

"So, babe, where do you see yourself in, like, five years?" I try to keep my tone as casual as possible. For as confident as I feel in our relationship, I negotiate for a freaking living. I understand how delicately these things need to be handled.

The corner of his mouth lifts into a smirk. "Living on my own private island in the middle of the Caribbean, working remotely and eating bonbons."

"I'm serious."

"Me too. I haven't been working my ass off for the past fifteen years to keep spinning my wheels in this rat race forever."

"Well, in this fantasy, am I with you on this private island?"

"Of course you are. Just you, me, and miles of

clear blue water."

Okay, not what I was expecting.

I take a sip of my water, doing my best to keep my cool. "Brian, you do realize that I'll be thirty-nine in five years, right?"

"Babe, you're beautiful. I've seen your mom, and honestly, you have nothing to worry about. I'm well aware of what happens to women's bodies with age."

"Does that include what happens to our eggs with age?"

He pauses, his eyes wary. "What do your eggs have to do with anything?"

I give him a forced smile. "Oh, I don't know. Maybe with the whole *getting pregnant and having babies* thing?"

"Oh." He sets his fork down and stiffens as he meets my eyes. "I, uh, I never really saw kids in my future."

Wait, what?

You've got to be fucking kidding me.

Trying to calm myself, I take a deep breath. Maybe it's not as bad as it sounds. Maybe we can work through this. "Okay . . . what does that mean?

Like you haven't thought about it before, but are open to it?"

"No, that means that I don't want them. I'm sorry, Layne, I guess I thought . . . well, I didn't think you wanted them either."

Gulping the last of my champagne, I stare up at the ceiling, tears stinging the corners of my eyes. *Stupid, Anderson, stupid. Pull yourself the hell together.*

I look back at him, my eyes narrow and my voice tight. "What makes you think I didn't want kids?"

He shrugs. "You're such a high-powered, no-nonsense, driven woman. I thought if you hadn't had any by now, it meant you weren't interested."

"You can have career ambitions *and* want a family. It's not the 1950s." My voice is stern, and my eyes are still narrowed.

"Well, I know that. I guess I just assumed you had your priorities straight."

Shocked, I try not to gasp, unable to believe what I'm hearing. "My priorities straight? Are you kidding me? What is wrong with you?"

Brian looks dejectedly down into his plate, and suddenly, I feel the whole night crumbling around me—and our relationship with it. I was wrong. So wrong. How could I be so horribly, terribly wrong about so many things?

"I'm sorry. I'll never want kids," he says, his eyes trained on his half-eaten bass.

"Well, I do," I reply, sitting up straighter and tossing my hair over my shoulder. "I always have."

"I guess that's it, then. I'm sorry, Layne, I really am." He stands, places a hundred-dollar bill on the table, kisses me on the cheek, and walks out of the restaurant.

My mouth falls open and tears well up in my eyes. Suddenly, I feel like I've been punched in the stomach and slapped across the face at the same time.

Before I fully lose it in public, I flag down our waiter and hand him more than enough money to cover the rest of the bill. He looks confused but sympathetic, asking no questions as I practically sprint out of the restaurant, wiping black mascara tears off my cheeks.

Once in my car, I pull my phone out of my purse and call the first number that comes to mind.

Half an hour later, I'm sitting on my couch, nursing a strong margarita in my comfiest pair of yoga pants, when a knock on the door pulls me out of my self-pitying trance.

My first thought is that it might be Brian, crawling on his hands and knees, begging me to take him back. But I know that won't be the case. Brian isn't the begging type. Besides, he made his position perfectly clear. There's no room to compromise on bringing another human into the world.

As I go to answer the door, I figure it's probably Kristen. When I called her on the drive home, I insisted she didn't need to come over, and the best thing for me would be to just drink alone and wallow. Maybe she saw through all that. Maybe she's worried about me and wants to make sure I don't drink myself into a coma. Either way, no matter how sure I was half an hour ago that I wanted to be alone, I have to admit that a little company sounds nice right about now.

"Look, Kris, you didn't have to come over—" I say, stopping mid-sentence once I swing the door open.

Because it's not Kristen standing there. It's Griffin, with a bottle of top-shelf tequila in one hand and my favorite margarita mix in the other. Dressed in dark jeans and a leather jacket with a white T-shirt underneath, he looks undeniably good.

Standing here in my ratty old oversized law school sweatshirt, I kind of wish I were more of a sexy loungewear kind of girl. But it's Griffin. He's definitely not someone I need to impress.

"What are you doing here?"

"Krissy told me what happened between you and the ass-wipe. I thought you could use some cheering up."

Oh. I can't help the soft pang inside my chest. "How did you know I was drinking margaritas?"

He smiles, cocking his head to the side and raising an eyebrow. "As far as alcohol goes, you're pretty fucking predictable, Anderson."

I scoff, crossing my arms and shifting my weight from one foot to the other. Griffin is the last person I was expecting to see right now but I'd be lying if I said I wasn't happy to see him.

"Come in."

I step out of the way as he breezes past me, the scent of his cologne washing over me. While I'm not usually a fan of masculine colognes, I'm surprised to find that I don't mind his smell. It's familiar. Comforting, even. Sandalwood. Lavender.

Safety.

"I didn't realize you were a fan of the *Real Housewives of Atlanta*," he says, setting the bottles on the kitchen counter and nodding to the TV playing loudly in the living room.

Quickly grabbing the remote, I switch over to an internet radio station, clicking on the first thing that pops up. "Today's Top Hits" starts playing through the mounted speakers as I shrug in his direction. "I just needed evidence that my life could be much, much worse."

"Living in a multimillion-dollar mansion with the ability to fulfill your every fleeting desire is worse than this?" He takes a quick, sweeping glance around my loft, which, to be fair, is no mansion.

But still, I bristle. "Hey, I worked hard for this place. It's prime real estate in this neighborhood."

He crosses his arms, arching a brow at the pile of dirty dishes in my sink. "If you were a Real Housewife, you'd pay someone to handle that shit for you."

"I can handle that shit myself, thank you very much. Go easy on me . . . I just got dumped by the man I thought I'd spend the rest of my life with."

"From what Krissy told me, it sounds like it was more of a mutual thing than a full-on dumping."

"Does it make a difference? I want kids, and he doesn't. Actually, it's worse than that. I want kids, and he thinks wanting kids makes me some weak, emotional, antiquated woman. How fucked up is that?"

Griffin slices a lime he found in my fridge into wedges and pours us each a drink, a blessedly strong one. But before he hands me my margarita, he pulls two shot glasses from the back of my cabinet and fills them to the brim.

I smirk as he slides a shot my way. "Is that what they're teaching you in graduate school? To start every evening with a shot?"

"Only when there's a damsel in distress."

"Please don't tell me that makes you my knight in shining armor."

He smirks. "If the shoe fits . . ."

"Shut up and take this shot with me," I say as I roll my eyes.

The clear liquid burns as it slides down my throat, the sour bite of lime afterward a welcome relief. I cough a little once my airway clears, and

Griffin smiles at me from across the counter. When I give him a reproachful look, he backs off, raising his hands in surrender. We take one more shot before bringing our margaritas to the couch, where I curl up in the corner, resting my head on my favorite fuzzy blanket.

"This is nice," Griffin says, draping his arm over the back of the couch and resting an ankle on his knee.

"Is this how you spend all your Saturday nights? Comforting your older female friends who've just been dumped?" I ask before taking a long sip of my drink. "You were always too good for him, you know. Sometimes what feels like an ending is actually a new beginning." He places a hand on my knee as his blue-green eyes meet mine, and it takes all my strength not to burst out laughing.

"How often does that line work?"

"More often than you'd think." His eyes soften, crinkling a little at the corners before he fires a cheeky wink my way.

This time I can't help it. I roll my eyes.

"If you came here looking for a pity lay, you've come to the wrong place."

His jaw ticks. "What makes you think all I'm

looking for is a lay?"

I pause at his question. The seriousness and determination in his tone confuses and intrigues me at the same time. The look on his face is sure. Confident. "Why are you here, Griff?"

He shifts, turning his hips so he's facing me straight on, his whole body aligned with mine. He takes my hand in his, running his thumb along my knuckles before meeting my eyes again. "I've never hidden the fact that I care about you, Layne. That's why I'm here."

Softening, I smile. "I'm sorry for making insinuations. God, I must sound like a bitch. Honestly, I'm glad you came. I realized after I hung up from Kris that I didn't want to be alone."

He lets go of my hand and picks up his drink again. "Yeah, when my sister hung up, I knew one of us needed to come over. She insisted you wanted to be alone, but I wasn't buying that for a second."

"Smart man." I nod, taking another sip of the deliciously crisp drink.

"It's not my first rodeo." He grins.

I throw the remote at his head. "Are you referring to my six breakups in the year before Brian?"

His lips twitch. "Maybe."

I take a deep breath and let my head drop back against the couch. He's right. I've been through my fair share of men in my hunt for Mr. Right, and Kristen and Griffin have had a front row seat to all my dating disasters. Brian seemed the most normal of the bunch and to be honest on paper we looked like the perfect match. We're both lawyers. Both in our mid-thirties.

Ugh. I need to stop thinking about Brian.

"Onward and upward," I say, raising my glass to Griffin's.

After clinking our glasses together, we both take a sip as a comfortable silence settles over us. It's nice being with someone who just gets me, someone I don't have to pretend around.

"Are you that torn up about this guy?" Griffin asks, his dark brows pushing together.

I take a moment to consider his question, and examine how I actually feel right now. And when I do, I begin to realize that it's not my heart that hurts. It's mostly my ego. I'm mad at myself that I wasted so much of my time on Brian before I figured out we weren't right together.

But after all the dating mistakes I've made, I thought it wise not to spring the baby thing on a man on one of our first few dates. And by then,

Brian and I had clicked so well and were operating on the exact same page, that I never even bothered bringing it up. I thought it was a forgone conclusion. He told me all the time how glad he was that he found me.

"I just feel like I wasted so much time when I really don't have time to waste. I know my soul mate is out there somewhere, you know?" I swallow, a fresh wave of emotion hitting me. "It just sucks."

Griffin frowns as he gazes at me. "You have nothing to worry about, Layne. You're gorgeous, successful, and—"

I hold up one hand, stopping him. "I have everything to worry about. I'm thirty-four years old. If I don't have a baby soon, I may lose my chance for good. Did you know that a woman's reproductive health declines drastically at age thirty-five?"

I expect him to make some noise of agreement or sympathy, or maybe offer a bit of encouragement. Instead, his face contorts into a frown.

"That's what this is about?" he asks, a line forming in his forehead. "Your desire to become a mom?"

I nod. "Of course."

"Fuck, okay then, that's easy." He blows out a breath as he says this. Then he leans forward, meeting my gaze with a serious expression. "Let me give you what you want. I can put a baby in you."

The tequila must be hitting me harder than I thought, because I think Griffin just suggested he be my baby daddy. There's absolutely no way he suggested that. But one look at his face tells me this has nothing to do with tequila and he is dead serious.

I sit there for a moment in stunned silence. Then my hazy, alcohol-soaked mind starts going a mile a minute, racing with all the reasons this is a very bad, very crazy idea.

"Griff . . ."

He grins wickedly. "Fully functioning baby maker," he points to his crotch, "right here."

I roll my eyes and chuckle at him.

"Look, before you say anything, hear me out. I'm not saying we need to get married, or anything. Hell, you don't even have to date me and I can simply be Uncle Griffin. You said your clock is going to run out in a few years, and I know how important being a mom is to you. I could help. All I'm suggesting is a simple transaction that'll lead to something miraculous. The oldest one in the book, really."

I stare at him, barely able to comprehend the words coming out of his mouth. *Is he actually serious? There's no way he's serious.*

"Griff, you're an idiot. A sweet one, but an idiot nonetheless."

He makes a small scoffing sound, collecting our empty glasses and taking them to the kitchen. "I'm going to pour us another drink. Just think about it," he calls over one shoulder before he steps out of view.

I shake my head, waving him away with the back of my hand.

It's not unusual for Griffin to be forward with me, whether it be with a corny pickup line or a full-blown come-on. But this? This is a whole other level. Of all the lines to try to get into my panties . . . a baby? Besides, he's still a college kid. Even drunk on a little too much tequila, there's no way I could ever take him seriously.

Plus, there's the not-so-little detail that I don't want to be a single mother. While I might be a strong, independent woman, I'm not one of those who thinks single motherhood would be a piece of cake. I work seventy hours a week and would need a support system. Tackling parenthood alone was never part of my plan.

When Griffin returns, he sits closer to me, so our legs are practically touching. He hands me my glass, and I drink, even though I know I should have stopped after the last one. But all memories of Brian must be erased, no matter how shitty I'll feel in the morning, so that's what I focus on as I continue drinking.

"Drink up, buttercup. And, seriously—the offer stands."

I take a sip and level him with a stare. "That offer being your sperm, just so I'm clear?"

He chuckles and flashes me a sexy smile. "Exactly."

I ignore him, as I often do, and merely smile back, but I can't ignore that tight feeling inside my chest.

Griffin laughs, tipping his drink toward his full lips. "What? I'm guessing I have very strong swimmers."

He's gorgeous, but he's also ten years younger than me and a cocky playboy. He can't possibly know what he's saying, offering to *put a baby in me*. I would never even consider it. Still, he's sweet . . . in a misguided, juvenile kind of way.

I've polished off half my drink before I realize that I need to slow the heck down. I'm already halfway to Drunkville and when I arrive in Drunkville all bets are off.

"So, tell me, Griffin, how'd you get so sweet?" The words slip out before I can think about them, my body leaning into his, and it's my first warning that I'm not halfway to Drunkville, I'm already there.

"Just born that way, I guess. Having an older sister helped too." His gaze lazily roams my face, moving from my hair to my eyes before settling on my lips.

"Are you this sweet to all the girls?"

He doesn't reply, slowly shaking his head and tucking a stray hair behind my ear.

His fingers are warm and soft as they graze my skin, sending a shock wave straight through my chest. Without thinking, I bring my mouth to his, our lips merely brushing at first. We hold still, his warm breath grazing my lips, electricity pulsing between us.

"Layne?" he whispers, his mouth still hovering over mine.

"Kiss me," I whisper back.

He moves closer until our lips touch—tentative at first, and then with growing urgency as he takes control of the kiss. He tastes like tequila and youth.

God, why can't I just throw caution to the wind for once?

Our mouths crash together, my hands hungrily raking over his firm chest. Holy hell, he's so solid. Every inch of me lights up with the need for his touch, my body suddenly aching for more. His hand cups my jaw, and he tilts my head, lining up our mouths as he deepens the kiss, his tongue eagerly tasting mine.

Hello, hormones. It's either the alcohol playing tricks on me, or Griffin is by far the best kisser I've ever had.

With a hungry groan, I crawl into his lap and straddle him. His hands move up my spine, and I feel the evidence of his heavy arousal pressing between my thighs. *Holy hell.* Every muscle south of my belly button clenches at once. The man is obviously sporting a *serious* package.

Dear God, I shouldn't know that detail about Kristen's little brother.

His hands smooth over my hair as I grind against him, loving the low groan that escapes from deep within him. I peel his jacket off so I can feel the firmness of his muscles under his shirt, his pecs tensing beneath my touch. Every fantasy I've ever had about him comes rushing to the surface, starting from when we first met in my office over a year ago.

The more I remember, the more my need for him grows, and the more ragged my breathing becomes. My hands go straight for his jeans, searching out the button, and end up brushing his erection instead. It twitches against my fingers just as his thigh meets my center, causing a moan to escape from my lips.

I don't care if he's too young.

I don't care if he's in college.

I don't care that he's my best friends little brother.

Right now, in this moment, there's only one thing I can think.

More.

I want more.

SIX

Griffin

Have you ever wanted something for so long, and when you get it, it's even better than you could have imagined?

Yeah. That's exactly how it feels to finally have Layne in my lap, grinding against me like her life depends on it. Our mouths are fused together in a hungry kiss, and her full, soft lips coax my tongue into her mouth and I'm more than happy to oblige.

She moves to kiss along my neck, her lips moving over the stubble of my jaw and then back down. I groan at the feel of her mouth on my skin. How did she know my neck is my secret weak spot?

As she runs a hand up my chest, I pull her hips, bringing her closer against my erection, and she inhales sharply as my full length presses into her. She leans into me, grabbing my shoulders, and uses the leverage to grind against me, giving me a small smirk before kissing my lips again, gently biting my lower lip.

Clearly, she likes to be in charge in the bedroom as much as she does in real life, and there's no way in hell I'm going to complain. The little moaning sounds she's making as she writhes against me are about to completely push me over the edge.

A year of wanting her and running through every possible fantasy is finally paying off—I know exactly what I want to do with her. I can't help but touch her, and my hands explore her curves, lingering on her full breasts. Thrilled to learn she's not wearing a bra beneath her sweatshirt, I run a thumb firmly across her nipple, eliciting a needy whimper that nearly makes me come in my jeans. *Fuuck.*

She feels so perfect in my arms, and the pressure of her rocking against me is heaven. This is everything I've ever wanted, but an annoying little voice in the back of my mind is telling me the timing isn't right.

"Layne," I say quietly, pulling back. "Wait."

Still straddling me, she sits up, her lips parted in confusion. We're both breathing heavily, and the sight of her chest rising and falling sends an ache to my groin that makes what I'm about to do all that much harder.

"Was I doing something wrong?" she asks, her emerald eyes glittering with desire.

"No, you're perfect," I say, using all my will-power to lift her off my lap. There's still a pulsing between my legs, but I swallow hard and keep my resolve. "But you're drunk. I don't want you to do something you'll regret in the morning. Fuck it'd kill me if you regretted anything you experience with me."

She laughs, shaking her head. "Come on, I'm an adult. I can handle my liquor. I'm not going to regret it," she says, reaching for the button of my jeans again.

"Layne, I'm serious." I grab her hand and meet her eyes with a serious expression, hoping I'm not ruining the already very slight chance I have of being with Layne in the future.

"Seriously? You hit on me for over a year, and now you decide to be a Boy Scout?" Frowning, she slumps back on the couch. "Weren't you offering me your sperm, like, thirty minutes ago?"

I stay silent, watching her. Even in an old sweatshirt, her eyes puffy from crying, Layne looks beautiful. Her dark hair is swept up in a ponytail that highlights her high cheekbones, which are flushed from our kiss.

She glances at me again, and her face softens. "I guess I did drink half a bottle of tequila. You're probably right," she says with a sigh, then gives me a sly look. "For once."

I laugh, rising to my feet in front of her, and take a deep breath to try to cool off. "Let's get you to bed," I say, holding out a hand to help her off the couch.

She leans on me as we walk to her room, and I can't help but smile. Confident, capable Layne is relying on me for once. And it feels pretty damn good. Like she trusts me. Maybe even needs me. When we get into the bedroom, she pulls out a white tank top and a pair of boy shorts, and I raise an eyebrow at her.

"What?" she asks, her face composed into a look of mock innocence. "In case you didn't notice, I spilled half of my last margarita down my sweatshirt. I can't sleep in wet clothes. Now turn around."

I turn so I'm facing the doorway and listen as Layne pulls off her yoga pants and sweatshirt. *Jesus*. She's less than ten feet away from me, almost completely naked. The universe is really testing me right now. But I know that she's only coming on to me like this because she's drunk, and the only thing worse than not being with Layne at all would be for her to regret it or feel taken advantage of. *Breath, Griff. You've got this.*

I try not to imagine how she looks in the skimpy tank top and panties, and let out a sigh of relief when I finally hear her climb into bed, the blankets rustling around her.

"Okay, you can look," she says, and I turn to find her underneath several blankets, her hair now loose around her shoulders.

"Don't fall asleep yet," I tell her.

She nods, sitting up against her pillows, and the blanket slides down enough to reveal the top of her breasts. I swallow hard and look away. *Not the time to get all hot and bothered again*, I think, turning to leave the room.

I head into the kitchen and fill a glass with water, then stop by the bathroom, searching through her medicine cabinet to grab a few Advil. When I get back into the room, Layne's eyes are closed, and she looks shyer and more innocent than I've ever seen her before.

"Hey," I say, gently touching her shoulder. "Before you go to sleep, you need to drink this. And take these. You'll thank me tomorrow, trust me."

She blinks her eyes open, groggily taking the water from me and swallowing the pills. Once she's had a few more sips of water, I set the glass on her bedside table.

"Why are you being so nice to me?" she asks as I move to turn off the bedside lamp.

I pause, gazing down at her. There are a million things I want to say, but none that I want to tell her when she just drank enough tequila to kill a small horse.

"If you think this is nice, just wait until I turn on the charm." I wink at her before turning out the light, press a kiss to her forehead, and shut the door.

I decide to stay over at her place, just in case. I'm sure she'll be fine, but I haven't seen someone down that much tequila since my first college frat party. I know I won't be able to sleep if I'm worrying that she's sick and needs help, so I set up a pillow and blanket on the couch.

As I pull the throw blanket over me and settle in, I can't help but smile. Even though I just had to basically beg the woman of my dreams not to sleep with me, I feel strangely happy and content. Being around Layne puts me at ease, and I like knowing that I can be there for her in a real way.

Tonight has taken some unexpected turns, but I wouldn't change any of it.

"Rise and shine," I say the next morning, pulling open the curtains so the sunlight spill into Layne's bedroom. It's already after ten, and I figure if I don't wake Layne up myself, she's going to stay in bed all day, wallowing in her hangover-induced post-breakup depression.

"My head feels like it's going to explode," she mumbles, pulling the blankets over her face.

"The best way to beat a hangover is to pretend you don't have one," I say with a smile, gently pulling the blanket off of her and handing her a sweatshirt and another two Advil.

She sits up, pulling the shirt on before swallowing the Advil with a gulp. Groaning, she lays her head back against her headboard.

"Are you always this cheerful in the morning?" she asks, shooting me a dirty look. "How does Kristen deal with you?"

I smirk at her. "Normally, I'd be offended by that, but I'll give you a pass since you've had a tough weekend."

As she climbs out of bed and grabs a pair of sweatpants from the floor, I catch a glimpse of her long, toned legs before she pulls them on, and my heart speeds up. I clear my throat, trying not to stare, but Layne doesn't even notice me as she stands up, yawning and stretching. Her hair is a mess and her eyes have that bleary, hangover look, but she could still turn heads.

Damn, how does she manage to look that good, even at her worst?

"First I get dumped, and now you won't even let me sit here and feel sorry for myself." She sighs, giving me a fake punch in the shoulder.

"First of all, you didn't get dumped. You made a mature decision to split with someone who couldn't give you what you wanted. And second, you're about to feel pretty bad for being such an asshole to me," I say, leading her to the kitchen.

She pads after me reluctantly, her eyes widening when she sees her kitchen table, where I've laid out a huge spread. I made my famous cheesy scrambled eggs, fresh-squeezed orange juice, and picked up coffee and muffins from the coffee shop down the street.

"Okay, I'm officially the worst," she says with a laugh as I hand her a latte and a plate.

"I got the biggest size they had," I say, gesturing at the coffee.

"You're amazing. Sunflower Café has the strongest espresso in town, bless them." She sips the latte gratefully before turning to me incredulously. "You made all this? Since when are you so domestic?"

"One of the perks of being a former party boy is that you learn all the best hangover cures," I say, ushering her into a chair. "Believe me, these scrambled eggs have gotten me through some of the roughest mornings of my life."

Layne snorts. "I can only imagine." She takes a bite of the eggs and her eyes light up. "How is this so good? Did you put crack in here or something?" she asks, forking another huge bite into her mouth.

"It's a trade secret," I tell her with a wink. "If you're lucky, I'll give you the recipe someday."

"Or you'll just have to come over here every time I'm hung over to make it for me," she says before sipping her orange juice.

"Deal," I say, grinning.

"I'm still in shock that you did all this for me. You're full of surprises, Griff." She looks into my eyes, holding my gaze for a few moments before she shakes her head and looks away. "But, seriously, thanks for all of this. It's so thoughtful. And I know I'm not exactly being Miss Sunshine right now."

I wave her concerns away. "Don't worry about it. I'm happy to help a friend in need."

"Speaking of our friendship," she says, setting her fork down.

Oh no, here it comes.

"About what happened between us last night. I'm sorry. I crossed a line."

I shake my head. "Layne, don't worry about it. We've all been there before. You were depressed and drunk. I just happened to be here, and you were looking for some comfort. Believe me, I get it."

Smiling, she nods. "Thanks for understanding. Having you here truly is helping. I almost don't feel like I want to throw myself off a bridge this morning."

"Anytime you need someone to give you back your will to live, you know where to find me," I say, lifting my glass of orange juice. She follows suit, and we clink glasses.

Frowning, she shakes her head at her plate. "God, I can't believe I wasted so much time on that guy."

"You want me to kill him?" I ask innocently, and she snorts.

"Could you?"

"Jokes aside, I'm always here for you, Layne," I say, looking into her bright green eyes.

She nods back at me. "I know, Griff. What would I do without you?"

I smile, and we finish eating in a comfortable silence.

So, maybe it's not exactly how I pictured my first time spending the night at Layne's, but I'm happier than I've been in a long time. Things between us may not be conventional, but somehow it feels right.

SEVEN

Layne

One year ago

The idling of a truck engine purrs outside, and I take a peek out the window. When I spot the rented moving truck stop beside the curb, I smile.

Right on time, a first for Griffin. For as long as I've known him, punctuality hasn't exactly been his strong suit. Honestly, it's amazing what having a serious girlfriend will do to a guy.

Standing and stretching my arms over my head, I take one last look around the nearly empty living room, cardboard boxes piled around the perimeter. When I closed escrow on my dream house last week, I thought the high of home ownership would be enough to carry me through the inevitable moving blues.

But no matter how excited I might be to be moving into my forever home—on my own dime, no less—I can't quite shake this gnawing feeling that something's missing. I guess I just thought that by the time I bought the home I planned to spend the rest of my life in, I'd have someone to share it with.

But then again, not wanting to wait around for Mr. Right any longer is the exact reason I went ahead and put an offer down on the modern two-story Spanish-style home I'd been eyeing for months. It's my life, whether it looks the way I thought it would or not. And there's no damn way I'm going to waste another second of it letting myself feel broken or incomplete.

"Morning," Griffin says cheerfully as he walks through the door, his turquoise eyes sparkling like they always do when he's in a playful mood. "You ready to do this thing?"

I'm glad to see he's in such good spirits this morning. Spending your day off helping a friend move shouldn't rate that high on weekend priorities.

"So ready," I say. "But, seriously, thank you for offering to drive the moving truck. I'd do it myself, but the thought of navigating that thing down Sunset Boulevard nauseates me."

He grins. "Don't thank me until we get all your shit where it needs to go in one piece."

"Do you really have that little faith?" I ask as I bend down to heft a box of old law books onto my hip. As I lift the box, the books slide to the other end, shifting the weight away from me and making it difficult for me to keep my grip.

Griffin quickly grabs the other end of the box, his eyebrows raising. "Why don't you let me do all the heavy lifting, okay?" he says, taking the box from my hands a little too easily.

"What, are you worried this old lady is going to break a hip or something?" I place my hands defiantly on my hips, but secretly, I'm relieved. The last thing I want to do is mortify myself further by throwing out my back or dislocating a disc. Then I'll really feel like a senior citizen.

"You've got to stop saying shit like that. You're thirty-six and that is definitely not old." Griffin's eyes are laced with concern rather than their signature playfulness.

"Yeah, well, let's see if you're still singing that tune once you hit thirty."

He shrugs and smiles, stacking the box of law books on top of another and carrying them both down to the truck. *Show-off.*

Griffin might be annoying, but I'm truly grateful he's here. Kristen and my mom offered to come by the new house and help arrange everything once it all gets there, but when it came to finding someone to help me actually transport my belongings, I figured I'd have to shell out a small fortune to a moving company. There was no one else to call. But then Griffin overheard my plan and insisted on being the one to help.

Over the past couple of years, he's become someone I can depend on, especially since he starting dating Cora last year. Not only has having a girlfriend taken the majority of his attention off me and shifted it to someone else, but it's forced him to mature in ways he didn't even know he had to in his man-whore days. Not that he's totally grown out of all his bad habits. At the end of the day, Griffin is who he is. But lately, I've liked having that person around more and more.

Once he's loaded up all the boxes, we begin the careful process of moving the few pieces of furniture I decided to keep. A lot of things I bought new, like the dining table and my beautiful new oyster-colored sectional that I had delivered to the new house. But some things I couldn't bear to part with, like the antique bookcase I bought when I first moved to Los Angeles.

"This thing weighs like a thousand pounds," he says, straining to lift one corner of the bookcase and shaking his head.

"It'll be fine. We've got this," I reply, rubbing my hands together and stretching out my legs.

"Are you sure you don't want to try to sell it? Will it even fit in your new place?"

Now he's just being silly. My new place is over a thousand square feet bigger than my loft.

I stop stretching and sigh, running a hand over the back of my neck. "I know it's not the prettiest piece of furniture in the world. but this bookshelf was my first real possession, the first thing I picked out and paid for all on my own. I had to pay a hundred dollars extra for the guy to carry it up those stairs for me, but it was worth it because having it in my space made it finally feel like it was mine, especially once I'd filled it with my law books. And now that I'm moving into this new house, my dream home, the first place that's fully, completely mine . . . maybe it's silly, but it feels like this bookshelf has to be there."

He nods, his eyes trained on the grayish wood, but I can't tell if he's sizing it up or getting ready to throw it out the window. Suddenly, without warning, he lifts the bookcase, groaning a little under the weight, then hefts the thing out my front door and lugs it down the stairs.

"Wait, Griffin—don't hurt yourself!" I call after him, following him down the stairs and hovering my hands around the top of the shelf, stunned by his stupid, if not sweet action.

Miraculously, he gets the thing down the stairs and into the truck all on his own, his biceps bulging beneath the sleeves of his T-shirt and sweat beading on his forehead. He groans loudly once it's loaded, panting and leaning against the cool metal of the truck. I stand in front of him, my arms crossed and eyebrows knit together, waiting for him to explain himself.

"What?" he asks, still struggling to catch his breath.

"Don't *what* me. Are you trying to kill yourself?"

He shrugs. "The bookcase is important to you. I found a way to get it down the stairs."

"I could have helped, you know."

"You said you paid the guy who sold it to you extra to get it up there, all by himself. I figured that meant I'd be able to get it down without help on my own too."

"If you think I'm paying you a hundred dollars for that, you're mistaken." I scoff, shifting my weight from one foot to the other and tossing my hair over my shoulder.

"You'll find another way to repay me." He winks, wiping the sweat from his brow with the back of his sleeve. The hem of his T-shirt lifts slightly with the motion, giving me a quick sneak peek of his abs, still as tanned and rippling as ever.

Jeez. It's not even fair.

My stomach cartwheels at the sight, and suddenly I remember how often he's showed up to our group hangouts, sweaty and gross from lifting at the gym. He's a strong guy; he knew he could handle the bookcase. And I should have known that too. So, why was I so worried about him hurting himself?

Before I can consider the question any further, Griffin claps his hands, assessing all the boxes and furniture he's perfectly Tetrised into the truck.

"Is this everything?" he asks, tucking a misaligned box back into its stack.

"I think so. But I'll go do one last walkthrough."

Climbing the stairs to my third-floor walkup for the last time, I think about all the memories I'm leaving behind here. All the girls' nights I've had with my friends, all the boyfriends who've passed through, all the times I tried to cook myself a nice meal and almost burned the place down.

I spent a good chunk of my twenties and thirties in this apartment, but I can say with confidence that now feels like as good a time as any to let it go. Tossing the keys on the kitchen counter, I wave good-bye to my old space, feeling a strange mix of calm and anxiety over seeing it all hollowed out.

I walk back outside to find Griffin leaning against the side of the truck, scrolling through his phone. He looks up and smiles when he hears me coming, tucking his phone into his back pocket.

"You ready?" he asks.

"As I'll ever be."

It's not a long drive to my new place, but in typical LA fashion, traffic turns what would be a fifteen-minute drive into a forty-five-minute one, giving the two of us plenty of time to catch up.

"So, how's Cora?" I ask. "Still studying for the LSAT?"

"Yeah, she's planning on taking it next month.

Thanks again, by the way, for lending her your old study materials. She says they're really helping."

"Of course. I'm always happy to support women in law."

"She asks about you all the time, you know, wanting to know where you started, how you opened your own firm so young, that sort of thing. It's kind of weird, actually." He glances over at me, his brows scrunching together.

When Kristen told me about Griffin's new girlfriend, I was surprised to hear she wanted to be a lawyer—and not just because he usually went for women with less ambition. The more Kristen told me about Cora, the more she sounded . . . well, familiar.

"She's probably just looking for a mentor. I'd be happy to meet with her, if that's something she wants."

"No, that's okay. I mean, I'm sure she'd love that, but I wouldn't want to impose."

"It sounds like you don't want me to meet your girlfriend." Griffin doesn't respond, staring straight out the windshield, drumming his fingers on the steering wheel, and an unfamiliar feeling tingles in my belly.

"Do you not want me to meet her?" I press, crossing my arms and shifting in my seat, my eyes widening slightly. "Are you worried I won't like her? Or that she won't like me?"

I've always introduced him to the guys I was dating over the years—if they stuck around long enough to meet my friends, that is.

He stays silent, chewing his lip and pointedly avoiding eye contact, pretending to be hyper-focused on the stop-and-go traffic ahead of us.

"Well, I hate to break it to you, mister, but I'm going to have to meet her sooner or later. You can't hide her away forever."

He finally speaks. "We'll see about that."

Shaking my head, I turn to look out my window, bothered by how weird Griffin is acting.

Is he embarrassed about being friends with a woman ten years older than him? That can't be it; he just said that she's impressed by what I do. Does he think I'll be rude and judgmental with her? Sure, I can be hard to please sometimes, but surely he's not under the impression that I would be anything but sweet to his girlfriend. Not that any of them have ever stuck around long enough for me to meet them before.

Maybe that's what it is. He's not used to having to introduce a girlfriend to his friends. That, I can understand. That makes sense to me, even if it does hurt my feelings a little.

By the time we finally make it to my new house, Kristen and my mom are already there, chatting away in the driveway, and they wave when they see us pull up. When my mom waggles her eyebrows suggestively at the sight of Griffin in the driver's seat, I roll my eyes. I love my mom, but she can be such a flirt sometimes, especially when it comes to young, attractive men. Thankfully, he's too busy trying to back the truck up to the curb to notice her gawking at him.

"Took you guys long enough," Kristen says as we climb out of the truck, pulling me in for a congratulatory hug.

"There was an accident on Sunset. Thankfully, my driver here handled it like a champ," I say, smiling gratefully at Griffin, who simply nods in response.

"I'm so proud of you, sweetheart!" My mom squeals, wrapping me in the tightest hug she's given me since I graduated from law school.

I hug her back, stifling an exasperated groan. "Thanks, Mom."

When I told her I was moving, she insisted on helping me move in, no matter how many times I told her it wasn't necessary. She's been itching for grandkids from the moment I got my first period, and it's no secret she's heartbroken that her only child is still single and childless at thirty-six. That being said, her sadness over my situation has recently turned into full-blown pity, hence the reason she insisted on being here to help me decorate. I know she means well, but my mom can be fucking depressing sometimes, even when she's trying to be upbeat and supportive.

Regardless, I won't let that dampen my spirits. I still can't believe I bought my own home. There's a sense of accomplishment about it.

Truthfully, I just thought it was time. I didn't need a husband in order to buy my own house. And a few months later, I'd gotten a mortgage, and a realtor. Now, *bam*, here we are today.

"Griffin, if I'd known you were going to be here and so helpful, I would have brought some leftovers for you to take home," my mom says after letting me go, turning her attention to an equal parts charmed and amused Griffin.

"That's all right, Mrs. A. I'm not a college student anymore. I can forage for myself," he replies with an easy smile that immediately wins my mom over.

"Well, from what I hear, you've got a new woman to cook for you. Coral? Clara?"

"Cora," he says, his smile fading slightly. "She's not much of a cook either, actually, but we're both experts at takeout and ordering in."

"Just like my Layne," my mom says, wrapping her arm around my waist and giving me a gentle squeeze.

I laugh along with her, but judging from the look on his face, Griffin isn't too pleased with the comparison. He forces a small chuckle, then gets to work unloading boxes from the back.

We work straight through the rest of the morning, getting everything out of the truck and into the house before I start directing them to the different rooms where each box needs to end up. It's trickier work than I imagined, even without doing any of the heavy lifting. The mental gymnastics is work enough, trying to decide what should go where, and figuring out what items I still need to make the place feel finished.

I've never had so much freedom in a living space, both in terms of square footage and ownership. And while I love having the ability to do whatever I want, whether that means which rug to place on the Mexican tile or painting the guest bathroom hot pink, after two hours of decision-making, I'm totally wiped out. It isn't until my stomach starts to growl that I realize it's time for lunch.

But before I can ask if anyone else is hungry, Griffin appears in the doorway, bulging plastic bags in hand. From the smell alone, I can tell he went to my favorite sandwich shop, and my mouth immediately starts watering.

"When did you leave?" I ask as Kristen and my mom wander in from the other room.

"Not long ago. You guys were busy with the master bedroom, so I figured I'd sneak out and get lunch." He leads us into the dining room and lays our food out on my brand-new mahogany table.

"Wait, Griff, did you put the table together?" I can't hide the shock or appreciation in my voice. "Why didn't you ask for help? It looks amazing."

It does look incredible. It's been months since I ordered the table, and even longer since I saw it in the store, so seeing it now in my very own dining room is making me all kinds of emotional.

"Like I said, you guys were busy. I wanted to surprise you." He shrugs like it's no big deal.

"Wow, Griff, you outdid yourself," Kristen

says, slapping him on the back.

My mom shakes her head, tears welling up in her eyes at the sight of the table. "Oh, Layney, it's beautiful. You're doing such a good job with this place." She sighs, dabbing at the corners of her eyes.

"Well, I had some help from my favorite interior designer," I say, nudging Kristen in the ribs.

"All I did was tag along to the furniture stores you dragged me to."

My chest warms with pride and happiness, and before we all totally collapse into emotional messes, we agree it's time to eat. Griffin hands out bags of chips and sandwiches, clearly proud of himself for being so on top of it.

When it comes to my turn, his smile turns devilish. "Sonoma chicken sandwich, hold the tomatoes, with an extra side of poppy seed dressing. And don't forget your salt-and-vinegar chips," he adds, his turquoise eyes dancing with delight.

"How did you—"

"I only remembered because of how ridiculously detailed your order was." He hands me my food with a wink, breezing past me and taking a seat next to his sister at the dining table.

As I sit there with the three of them, eating my favorite sandwich from my favorite deli in all of LA, watching him chat so easily with my mom, I'm not sure this kind of attention is something I should get used to.

Especially with Cora in the picture. She seems good for him, and for as weird as he's been acting about her today, I think he really likes her.

No matter how much I've come to genuinely appreciate Griffin's friendship, it would be good for him to be in a relationship, and surely that means our close friendship will probably need some breathing room. I can't imagine his serious girlfriend being okay with him spending so much free time with another woman—even if it is strictly platonic.

I wouldn't want to do anything that would stand in the way of him becoming the man he's supposed to be. And based on what I've seen of him today, I'm excited to meet that man.

EIGHT

Griffin

After dropping off the moving truck and picking up my car, I drive back over to the new house to find Layne's mom and Kristen preparing to leave. The boxes have all been put in the right rooms and the furniture is assembled and in its place.

I'm genuinely happy for Layne that she finally has her dream house. She's always working so hard to make other people happy; it's nice to see her do something big for herself.

I climb out of my car and walk over to where the ladies are saying good-bye.

"Always a pleasure to see you, Griffin," Layne's mom says with a smile. "It's nice to know there's at least one helpful young man left in LA."

"Okay, Mom, time to go," Layne says, urging her toward her car as Kristen snorts out a laugh.

"I do what I can," I say with a wink at her mom. I always get a kick out of older women hitting on me, and it's even better that it's Layne's mom.

"See you at home, Griff," Kristen says, fake punching me on the arm.

I stand in the driveway, waving as they climb into their cars and pull out. It's almost six in the evening, and my entire body feels beat. I hit the gym regularly, but moving furniture all day was a full-body workout. And I'd be lying if I said I wasn't trying to show off my strength, just a little.

Once the cars have faded into the distance, Layne moves toward the porch and collapses into one of her Adirondack chairs.

"So, how does it feel knowing that you're going to be sleeping in your very own house tonight?" I ask, following her lead and sliding into a chair. I made sure her bedroom was all set up before we called it quits.

A cool breeze blows by and I breathe it in, staring out at the sun that's quickly sinking.

"It feels pretty damn amazing," she says, turning to look up at the house. "Maybe not exactly how I pictured moving into my dream house, but I'm excited for this next chapter."

"What do you mean?" I ask, frowning. All I've heard for weeks is how excited Layne is to move into this place. I'm surprised to hear there's something she's unhappy about.

"Oh no, everything's great," she says quickly. "It's just . . . I don't know. I shouldn't complain. I have a great life, you know?"

"Layne, you know you can tell me anything, right? I would never judge you," I say, turning toward her.

She looks down, not quite meeting my eyes. "Well, I guess I just assumed when I moved into a home, it would be with—you know, a family." She sighs and bites her lip before looking up at me. "Does that make me sound totally pathetic?"

"No, it doesn't," I tell her honestly. "I know you want a family, but it's not like you can't still have all that. You're just doing it in a different order than you thought."

She nods, but it's clear she's lost in her own thoughts. Finally, she says, "I guess I just feel like what's the point of working hard and having all this money if there's no one to enjoy it with?"

I reach over, taking her hand in mine. "Believe me, you'll have someone to share it with. You're amazing, but these things take time but one day you'll get everything you want".

Layne smiles, then shakes her head. "You're right. I think I'm just tired."

She stands up and stretches.

"I guess this was a little more than you signed up for when you offered to help me move," she says with a laugh, then glances around. "It's such a nice night. Do you want to hang out and have a drink in the backyard? I promise I'm done being all moody and existential."

Unsure, I hesitate. I have plans to meet up with Cora for a movie night, and two minutes ago I was planning to leave. But now I don't feel so good about skipping out and leaving Layne alone in this big house when she's feeling vulnerable.

"Yeah, a drink sounds great." I pull out my phone and shoot off a quick text to Cora.

Gonna be a little late. Can we start movie night later?

I ignore the twinge of guilt I feel as I follow Layne inside, where she pulls out tequila and margarita mix.

"Some things never change," I say with a grin as she mixes up two perfectly crafted margaritas.

"I'm a woman who knows what she likes," she says, handing me an icy drink with a smile.

I follow her into the backyard, where earlier I assembled a new patio set. It's the time of night when the sun has set just enough to cool things off. Layne plugs in the string lights we looped around the fence earlier, giving the space a warm glow. It's quiet in the yard, other than the sound of far-off cars.

Layne runs her fingertips over the back of one of the black iron chairs before sinking down into its plush cushioned seat.

"I've always thought of myself as an apartment kind of guy, but I could get used to this lifestyle," I say, leaning back in my own chair. "You did good finding this place, Anderson."

"It's pretty great, isn't it? This yard is what sold me on the house." She sips her drink and lets out a sigh, pulling her dark hair out of the confines of the ponytail she's had it secured in all day.

Dressed in jeans and a white T-shirt, with her hair loose and wild, she looks younger than her birth certificate claims. Even if I was friend-zoned a long time ago, it's difficult not to notice how gorgeous Layne is. I don't see that changing anytime soon, whether I'm dating someone or not.

I'd never cheat or do anything to break Cora's trust, but that doesn't mean I can just turn off the feelings I have for Layne. The hot encounter we had on her couch after her last breakup didn't help the lustful thoughts I still secretly harbor.

The way she moved against my lap, the soft, need-filled sounds she made that went straight to my groin, the way she kissed, like she was all in and ready for whatever I could give her . . . They're only things I let myself think about late at night when I'm alone. And when those memories do invade my brain, my hand usually makes its way under my briefs for a quick jerk session.

Layne would kill me if she knew I still thought about that night, and Cora would definitely dump my ass. Which is why I should suppress those memories. But it's easier said than done, especially now, watching Layne lick an icy droplet of lime from her plump bottom lip, and run her fingers through the long lengths of her tangled hair.

"I'm thinking about having a housewarming party. Maybe then I can finally meet your mysterious girlfriend," she says, wiggling her eyebrows as she sets her drink on the glass-topped table.

Cora.

Right.

My girlfriend.

Deciding it's time to remove myself from further temptation, I stand up and stretch. "I should get going."

"Are you sure?" Layne asks. "I've got that whole bottle of tequila. Don't make me drink it alone."

"Believe me, the last thing I want to do is facilitate another tequila binge, but I'm late to meet Cora," I say, grinning at Layne. "We have big plans to watch *Psycho*. Can you believe she's never seen Hitchcock?" I shake my head in mock disappointment. "Kids these days."

"Ah, okay," Layne says.

Something passes over her face that I can't quite place. But when I blink, she's smiling again, leaving me wondering if I imagined it.

She follows me inside where I set my empty glass in the sink. We walk to the front door together, and I take one last look around.

"This place looks really good," I tell her, smiling. "I have a good feeling about it."

Layne smirks at me. "I hope so, because I just sank a small fortune into buying it. Good luck with Cora's cinematic education," she adds, leaning against the door frame as I step out onto the front porch. "And thanks for helping me today. I know it was a lot."

"I was happy to help." As I give her a quick hug good-bye, I breathe in her familiar scent and then take a step back, releasing her.

I wave good-bye to Layne as I pull out of the driveway. Watching her turn to head back into her big, empty house gives me a sinking feeling in my stomach. But I shouldn't feel bad. Layne's an adult and doesn't need me to watch over her, but something about her seemed more vulnerable today than usual. Then again, why do I care so much? She's made it clear that she can handle herself.

My mind is still on Layne as I pull up to Cora's place. I stopped on the way to get her a *sorry I skipped out on our date* treat that will hopefully make up for not spending more time with her on her one free night.

I use the spare key to let myself into the apartment, calling out as I walk in.

"Hey, babe," I say into the hallway, but the apartment is silent. "I know I'm late, but I got your favorite chocolate chip cookies to make it up to you."

I step into the living room, where Cora is sitting on the couch, and get the sense that something's wrong. She's giving me a look I can't quite read. She sniffles quietly, and her eyes seem a little puffy.

"Cora, what's wrong?" I ask, quickly walking over to the couch to give her a kiss.

When she stares straight ahead without kissing me back, it confirms that something's wrong. She's usually the affectionate one when we see each other, and is almost never in a bad mood. One of the things I like about her is how upbeat she always is. It's freaking me out that Cora's like this, and I hope I'm not going to have to do damage control because I missed our date.

She gives me a strange look. "What happened? Where were you?"

"Didn't you get my text? I just got caught up with moving, and then Layne was upset, so I felt bad leaving her alone," I say, taking a seat next to Cora on the couch.

She turns to me, her brown eyes welling with tears. "Why couldn't Kristen stay with her?"

At the suspicion in her voice, I stiffen, furrowing my brow. "She and Layne's mom had already left. It just sort of came up as we were finishing moving. What's this about?" I ask gently. Whatever Cora's thinking, I don't want to escalate it by getting upset.

"I just don't see why you had to cancel our plans to spend more time with Layne. You know this is my one free night this week."

The coldness in Cora's voice makes dread settle into my stomach. Trying to keep my voice even, I say, "Look, Layne needed me. If a friend needed you, I'd never get mad at you for canceling our plans to be there for them."

The truth is, I feel totally blindsided. I don't get why Cora's being so weird about this. She's always saying how important it is that we have our own lives in addition to our life together.

"Are you sure you were just helping a friend tonight, Griff?" she asks, and her voice sounds like it's about to break. "Or is it more than that?"

Shit. So this is what's bothering her.

"Are you trying to insinuate that I'm cheating on you with Layne?" I ask in a measured tone. Trying not to get upset, I take a deep breath. I've never given Cora a reason to think I'd be unfaithful. I'm not the kind of guy who would do that, and the fact that she's suggesting I am hurts.

"No, Griffin, I don't think you'd cheat on me. You're a good guy," she says, and the look in her eyes is heartbreaking. "That's what makes this so hard."

"Makes what so hard? What are you trying to say?"

Cora lets out a long breath, brushing her dark hair back from her face. "When we were first dating and you'd always talk about Layne, I thought it was cute. I thought you just looked up to her or something, as your sister's successful best friend. But now I'm not so sure. You'll drop everything to spend time with her, even for something shitty like helping her move." She looks into my eyes as a tear runs down her cheek. "I think you're more into her than you are into me. I've thought it for a while. I just didn't want to admit it."

Totally dumbstruck, I stare at her. I had no idea she felt this way. I genuinely like being with Cora, but a little niggle in the back of my mind keeps me from denying what she's saying.

The truth is, I do still have feelings for Layne. I thought I just needed to meet someone else so I could get over her, but I've been with Cora for a while and nothing has changed.

Do I still want Layne? Abso-fucking-lutely. But will she give me the time of day? No, I'm sure she wouldn't. Which is why I moved on because what other choice did I have? But Cora's still staring at me, and my silence is all the response she needs.

"I'm not mad at you," she says, looking away. "I don't think you did any of this on purpose. But you can't be in a relationship with me when you're hung up on someone else."

Frustrated, I blow out a sigh. "I'm sorry," I tell her, reaching out to hug her good-bye. What else can I say? I feel like a total asshole.

"I just need to be alone right now," she says quietly.

I nod. My instinct is to try to comfort her, but I know that would only make things worse.

Overwhelmed by the thoughts swirling inside my head, I leave Cora's key on the kitchen counter and head home. When I woke up this morning, I would have never guessed the day would end with us breaking up. We seemed so solid.

At my place, I collapse onto my couch with a sigh, having to fight the urge to text Layne to talk this through with her. She's the only one who would know what to say to make me feel better, but she's the one person I can't call about this. Layne has made her feelings clear, and she's not interested in being with me. I don't particularly feel like being rejected twice in the same night.

Thanks, but no thanks.

NINE

Layne

One month ago

"Layne, I have Bob from Kincaid Incorporated on the phone. He has some questions about the merger."

Sabrina's light and cheery voice snaps me out of my email-answering-induced zombie state, and I instantly sit up straight, my brain struggling to focus. I chug the rest of my now-cold soy latte before pressing the button on the intercom to respond.

"Thanks, Sabrina. Put him through."

Within moments, my phone rings, and I wait a beat to pick it up. "Hi, Bob. What can I do for you?"

"Hi, Layne. Listen, I have some concerns about

this contract you sent over earlier. Are we actually going to give these guys the rights to fifty percent of our sales revenue moving forward? Doesn't that sound a little generous to you?"

I sigh, pinching the bridge of my nose. "I understand your concern, but that's the compromise we came to at our meeting last week. That's how we got them to agree to keep the name Kincaid on the title moving forward. If you'd like to renegotiate, we'll have to set up another meeting to get it sorted out."

"But isn't there some other way to keep my name without handing over *half* of our revenue?" His voice tightens, and I can imagine the vein in his forehead throbbing like it always does when he tries to keep himself from yelling. Bob's been a client for almost five years now, and anger management isn't exactly his forte. Which is exactly why he has me as an intermediary for this type of thing.

"That's certainly something we can explore, but again, we'll need to set up another meeting to discuss it with Saunders & Sons."

"Those greedy little fuckers . . ." He growls, his sentence trailing off into incoherent grumblings.

I roll my eyes, doing my best to keep my tone professional. "Is there anything else I can do for you today, Bob?"

"Well, if you could find a way to keep those assholes' hands off my money that would be great."

"Okay, I'll have Sabrina call Jillian and set up a meeting. I'm sure we'll find a solution that makes everyone happy."

"That's what you said a week ago, and yet here we are."

Taking a deep breath, I stand and start to pace, the gears in my brain cranking a mile a minute. "Bob, do you remember where your business was at when we started working together?"

"Well, we'd run into some hard times, sure, but it wasn't serious, by any means."

"No, you were drowning in legal fees. Your last corporate lawyer royally fucked you over, and that's why I always give you a pass for not trusting me."

"Come on, Layne. You know I trust you."

"No, you don't, and that's okay. Because I'll do my job, whether you believe I can or not. With my legal guidance, we turned your sinking business into a well-functioning, profitable enterprise in a matter of months. And this merger is the next step in securing a healthy financial future for your company for years to come. Do you want a healthy financial future for your company or not?"

"Well, of course I do."

"Good. We're on the same page then. Now, why don't you do your job, and let me do mine."

"Fine. I'll have Jillian set up a meeting."

"Great. Talk to you later." I hang up, yanking my earbud out of my ear and shoving my hands through my hair.

You'd think that after five years of working together, this asshole would get over the fact that I'm a woman and trust me to get shit done for him. But if this job has taught me anything, it's that the saying "you can't teach an old dog new tricks" still rings true in certain fields. And let's just say that Bob is a *very* old dog.

My office door cracks open and Sabrina pops her head through, gently knocking on the metal frame. I wave her in, aware of the subtle chastisement that's coming.

"*Royally fucked you over?* Since when is that the way you talk to clients?" she asks, her voice low and hushed. Her brows are raised so high, they practically disappear behind her thick auburn bangs.

"I needed to speak to him in the kind of language he can understand," I reply, plopping myself back down into my chair.

She holds up both hands. "You know I'm all for relating to clients on their own terms, but that kind of language is so out of character for you. Are you doing okay?"

"I'm fine," I say, waving her concern away and turning back to my computer.

I can feel her watching me in disbelief, but I ignore her stare. I don't have time to examine my behavior at work, and frankly, I think she's over-reacting.

Bob was one of my first clients on retainer when I opened my own firm. I'm always hard on him, and he's always hard on me. We hold each other accountable, and at the end of the day, whether it's pretty or not, we need each other. I know with every fiber of my being that he's not going anywhere.

"Whatever you say, boss. Don't forget you have lunch with Sadie in half an hour," she says on her way out, shooting me a reproachful look before shutting the door behind her.

Shit. I completely forgot.

Sadie's a friend from college who moved to the

area a few months ago, and while we hadn't kept in super-close contact since graduating, we've always been close. No matter how much time goes by, whenever we get together, it's like we just saw each other yesterday. Besides, after all the crazy shenanigans we saw each other through in our twenties, there's no way we could ever really stop being friends.

I shoot off a few more emails before grabbing my purse and hurrying to the parking lot, my stomach already growling. We're meeting at one of my favorite lunch spots a few minutes away from the office, and I can't wait to order my go-to salad—or to see Sadie, of course.

When I arrive at the warm, brightly lit café, I spot Sadie instantly, her signature waist-length dark hair swept over one shoulder. She's wearing a flowy, brick-red shift dress, the hemline hitting just below her knee, the color perfectly complementing her olive-toned skin. Her sense of style makes me I wish I'd worn something a little cuter today than my usual pencil skirt and blazer.

A smile brightens her face when she sees me, and she stands and wraps me in a huge hug that immediately reminds me why we're such good friends. Sadie is the warmest, kindest, most loving soul I've ever met, and being with her now makes me forget all the meaningless bullshit at work.

Thank God.

"Oh my God, Layne, it's so good to see you!" She squeals, stepping back and giving me a head-to-toe once-over. "You look amazing. I love the whole *corporate badass* look." She winks.

"Are you kidding? Look at you! I swear you haven't changed at *all* since college."

"Oh, please, you're being way too nice. After ten years of marriage, I've definitely gained a little comfort weight."

She giggles, and I laugh along with her, my eyes lingering on the silver band and round-cut solitaire diamond on her finger. Sadie was the first of all of us to get married, and I remember her wedding like it was yesterday. At that time, I was so sure I'd be right behind her walking down the aisle . . . and yet, here we are.

"Come on, you look amazing. When are you going to tell me the secret to keeping your hair so shiny and healthy?" I ask.

"Being Polynesian is a good place to start," she says, her deep brown eyes dancing with amusement. "But besides that, coconut oil works wonders."

We laugh again as a waiter appears at our table

with waters. Once he takes our orders—the Chinese chicken chopped salad for me, and a Cobb salad for her—we dive into catching up, eager to hear about everything we missed by not living in the same city.

"I still can't believe you opened your own firm," Sadie says, leaning forward and resting her chin on her palm, her eyes wide.

"It sounds a lot harder than it actually is. I was practically running the place at my last firm, and not getting paid for the work I was doing got old really fast. Once I found an office space that was affordable, the rest was history."

"You're a force, Layne. You really are."

"Stop it. What about you? A transfer to Los Angeles has to mean good things for you, right?"

"Well, I'm certainly not doing anything as exciting as running my own law firm, but yeah, it's kind of a big deal. I'd heard rumors months ago that they were looking for someone to replace the head of HR at the main office, but I swear, I never thought in a million years it would be me."

"But you've always been so good at what you do."

"Thanks. It's exciting, but I'm just hoping I

don't shatter all their expectations."

"You won't. I'm sure of it."

"Speaking of shattering expectations—did you hear about Alyssa?"

I shake my head, a small knot forming in the pit of my stomach. Alyssa is another of our married friends from college, one of the only ones to give up her career to stay home while her husband brings home the bacon. We've never been that close, but I've always liked her and often wonder how she's doing. Something tells me I'm not going to like what I'm about to hear.

Sadie's face is bright and excited. "You'll have to keep it on the down low because it's still early days, but she just found out she's pregnant! Can you believe it?"

I do my best to match her tone, but the knot in my stomach grows larger. "I didn't know she and Adrian were trying."

"They didn't tell anyone. I was sure they didn't want kids, they've been married for so long without them, but it turns out I was wrong. I saw her a couple weeks ago, and she's absolutely glowing." Sadie keeps talking, explaining how they'd been trying for a year and a half and were about ready to turn to IVF before Alyssa finally skipped a period and did an at-home test.

I plaster a smile on my face throughout the whole story, but on the inside, the knot in my stomach tightens, threatening to make me ill. I can practically feel the physical weight of my disappointment and shame pressing down on me, pinning me to the chair.

Eventually, I tune Sadie out, my thoughts spiraling out of control.

Alyssa is thirty-four and married, and even she considered turning to IVF. I just turned thirty-seven, hopelessly single, and totally at a loss as to how I'll ever find someone to settle down with. Now more than ever, the life I've always imagined for myself—where I'm happily married to the man of my dreams with a thriving career and a couple of kids—seems completely, absolutely out of reach.

When our food arrives, Sadie changes the subject. Still, the damage is done.

I barely taste my salad and go through the rest of the lunch in a daze, doing my best to fake being happy and content, but I know that I'm failing. Sadie doesn't say anything about it, but she gives me a worried look when we part, making me promise to call her next week to set a time to come have dinner at her place.

By the time I make it home from work later, I still haven't been able to shake the heavy feeling. If anything, it's gotten worse. Every email, every phone call, every meeting at work is like a reminder of all the time and energy I've spent on this part of my life—while totally ignoring the other goals and aspirations I had for myself.

After pouring a glass of red wine and plating a few slices of cheese, I settle on the couch. Sighing, I flip to something mindless on the TV so I don't feel so damn alone in this cavern of a home I was so sure would be filled with other people by now. I rifle through my drawer of takeout menus and decide on Indian food for dinner, but when I pull my phone out of my purse, it's already ringing. I'd forgotten to take it off DO NOT DISTURB after my lunch with Sadie, so I quickly answer, barely even glancing at the name on the screen.

"Hello?"

"Settle a bet for me. Are all corporate lawyers so busy they never call any of their friends back, or are you just one of those *out of sight, out of mind* assholes?"

I chuckle and roll my eyes. It's Griffin, busting my balls yet again for not calling him back a couple of days ago. "You'd think after four years you'd have learned by now that I don't call back unless you leave a message."

"Only a monster leaves their friends *voice mails*."

"Oh, so now I'm a monster? And you wonder why I don't call you back."

"I know for a fact my voice mail has been full for six months now. So either you're a liar, or I, like the good friend I am, always answer my phone."

"Uh-huh, sure, whatever you say." I let out a weak chuckle. "What do you want, Griff?"

"She's in a great mood today, folks," he replies sarcastically, making a clucking sound with his tongue.

I know he's only teasing me like always, but after the day I've had, I'm not really in the mood for it. "Let's just say it's been a day."

"Are you okay?" he asks, his tone serious now.

"Yeah, I don't know." I sigh. "I had lunch with an old girlfriend today and was reminded of all the parts of life I've let pass me by."

"I didn't know you had a questioning phase in

college," he teases. When I don't laugh, he sobers up again. "Sorry, you said girlfriend. I couldn't resist."

"No, it's fine. I just can't believe this is what my life looks like right now." I down the rest of my wine and pour another glass. If this gnawing, sinking feeling isn't going away on its own, I'm ready to drown it out, at least for tonight.

"You mean you can't believe that you're a high-powered lawyer living in the home of her dreams?"

He keeps his voice light and sort of teasing, but I can tell he's serious too. It's a sweet gesture, but not enough at this point.

"The home of my dreams includes the love of my life and the pitter-patter of little feet. Without all that, this place is just an empty shell."

I surprise myself with how depressing that sentence is. I can't remember the last time I felt this low, or if I ever really have before. Part of me worries about what it says about me that I'm not even trying to hide my sadness—but then again, this is Griffin I'm talking to. I'm not sure I can hide anything from him anymore.

When he doesn't respond for a few seconds, I check my screen to make sure the call hasn't dropped. "Griff? You still there?"

"Yep, sorry, I was checking something. What are you doing tomorrow?"

Figures he'd change the subject. He's twenty-seven. Not exactly an age where you're ready to deal with your older friends' existential dread.

"Oh, I don't know, what does any single thirty-seven-year-old woman do on a Saturday? Clean the bathroom? Adopt a cat or two?"

"Good. Clear your schedule. I've got something to cheer you up."

I chuckle at his misplaced optimism. "Look, that's sweet of you, but really, I'm fine. I think a quiet weekend in will help turn things around."

"I'll pick you up at ten. Pack an overnight bag—and don't forget a bathing suit."

"Wait. What are you—" But before I can ask my question, the line goes dead.

Did he hang up on me? I stare at the blank screen for a moment, trying to process what the hell just happened—and to formulate an excuse to get out of whatever trip he has planned for tomorrow.

Then again . . . did he say something about bathing suits?

My mind wanders to the last time I caught a glimpse of him shirtless. Maybe a year ago now? Maybe longer. The image is burned into my memory, one I revisit more often than I'd like to admit.

All right, fine. I'll give him a chance to cheer me up. Something tells me whatever Griffin has planned, I won't want to miss it.

TEN

Griffin

Compared to most people, yes, I am a very spontaneous person.

I'm usually the first to suggest skinny-dipping at a pool party. I'm not afraid to recommend some drunken truth or dare at a family reunion. True, there are certainly times when that impulsive decision-making bites me in the dick. *Hard*. And I'm afraid this might be one of those times.

"I'm so sorry about this weekend," I tell Wren, injecting equal parts regret and self-reproach in my voice.

I don't really *do* the regret thing, so it's harder than I remember. I'm also not very good at self-deprecation.

But it's always been easy lying to Wren, as shitty as that sounds. I've had to weasel my way out of more than one situation with the help of a little white lie, just to preserve something of *myself* every now and then. It's hard having a needy friend hanging on your arm every time you leave the house.

"I feel like a dick," I tell her.

"Your words, not mine," she snaps back, obviously pissed. "Just like last time, and the time before. What's going on with you?"

I've just told Wren that I can't go camping with her tonight. It's something we used to do in school, a whole group of us. And more often than not, Wren would get too drunk and find herself in my sleeping bag at the end of the night. Forgive me if I'd rather not spend the night curled up, sans blanket, on the dirt again.

"You know, ever since I split up with Cora, I've been scattered, and now a friend needs my help this weekend."

That isn't a lie. Being with Cora reminded me how much I want to be in a meaningful relationship. One with substance that's just about getting my dick wet on the regular. I want to spoil a woman, claim someone as mine, work toward a future, and more than anything, I want to find long lasting love. No matter how much I liked Cora and enjoyed her company, I knew she wasn't the one.

Now that I'm single again, I feel like an untethered buoy, bobbing around in the vast ocean of my empty sex life. I haven't slept with *anyone* since the breakup. Frankly, I don't even know if my dick is still down there. It's not that I don't have the urges . . . it's just that the one person I want refuses to see me as more than a fuckboy with little to no future. *Good times.*

"That was the whole point of this trip! To bring you back to the real you," Wren says with a moan.

Now *that* annoys me.

"Maybe I'm all over the place, but I feel more like myself than I have in months," I say calmly. It always bothers me when Wren thinks she knows me better than I do.

"I don't disagree with you," she says with an exasperated sigh, probably inspecting her nails like she does whenever she knows she's in the wrong but won't admit it.

Tired of this conversation, I say, "Look, I'll make it up to you, okay? We can do brunch next week."

"Brunch? Really, Griffin? Brunch is the go-to for when you *don't* want to hang out with someone."

"Not for me. Brunch is a marathon with me. We start with mimosas and end up at the corner bar six hours later."

Wren laughs. I think I've saved my ass, for now.

We say our good-byes, and I toss the phone on my couch. I need to shake off the whole unnecessary *thing* this friendship has become.

Why is talking to Wren such work sometimes?

It's not like that with Layne. With her, it can be a challenge, sure. But it's exciting and always new. Even after all these years we're constantly discovering new things about each other, for the better. There isn't any of this weird circular bullshit.

Thinking of Layne, I start packing. Sunbathing on the beach, roasting our dinner over a fire, sipping on margaritas as the sun sets over the crystal waters . . . I have a perfect vision for how I want this night to go.

Now I've just got to make it happen.

I hadn't forgotten what Layne's half-naked body looks like, but I appreciate the refresher.

Her hair falls in long, messy waves across one shoulder while the other is bare, enjoying its moment in the sun. Her bathing suit is fucking phenomenal—a navy-blue number, high waisted and cheeky, with a halter top that cups her breasts so perfectly, it's hard to keep my eyes where they belong.

Jesus, Griff. You need to get laid. But these aren't just any woman's tits . . . these are the tits of a woman who's placed me squarely in the friend zone.

"Hello? Eyes up here?" Layne waves in my face.

We're in our swimsuits on a surprisingly vacant beach, towels and cooler at the ready. I've been lying on my side, my head propped up on one hand, unabashedly staring at her gorgeous body. The sun is beating down on us, apparently frying my brain.

I protest, tapping her sunglasses with one finger. "What eyes? I don't see them."

Layne snorts, pushing her sunglasses up on top of her head. Her piercing green eyes meet mine, and awareness jolts through me.

Fucking hell.

"Better?" she asks.

"It'll do." I sigh, feigning nonchalance. "How are you feeling?"

"Better," she says with a smile. "I always forget how much sunshine can actually improve one's mood."

"Exactly. You just needed some vitamin D."

"Gross."

"Believe it or not," I say with a chuckle, "I wasn't making a dick joke."

"Not." She smirks and throws herself back on her towel, her breasts bouncing with the effort.

I can't tear my eyes away. *I'm such a perv.*

"It's so hot," she murmurs, placing her sunglasses back over her eyes, then trails her fingers across her collarbone, discovering the moisture there.

I almost offer to take care of that with my tongue, but think better of it. *Now's not the time, dude.* "So, are you going to tell me why you've been so depressed?"

She sighs dramatically. "People don't need a

reason to be depressed, Griffin. You really need to catch up on your mental health awareness."

"Maybe," I reply, my brow furrowed, "but I know you. And I know that you usually have a reason for feeling down."

Layne turns her head toward me, biting her lip. It's clear she's deciding whether she wants to share what's on her mind.

I'm careful not to change my expression. My impulse is to try to make her laugh, to erase those worry lines from her face. But I need her to know that I'm serious, and that I legitimately care about what she's going through.

"It's nothing new," she finally says with a soft sigh. "I just found out that one of my close friends from school is pregnant. I didn't even know she wanted kids. She was one of the only ones left that hasn't already had them. And now . . . well, now it's just me."

Her voice cracks on those last words, and I see a tear race down her cheek from under her lenses, too fast for her to catch. I reach over, using the back of my fingers to wipe it away. She smiles at me, but her expression is still sad.

"I should just be happy for her," she says, trying to lighten the mood with a choked laugh.

"I'm sorry," I whisper. I can't even imagine how difficult this news must have been for her. Knowing Layne, she's been trying to push it down and not deal with the negativity she must be feeling. "It's okay to be happy and sad at the same time."

"Is it?" she asks.

Is she really asking me? Or is this one of those rhetorical lawyer things? I take a chance.

"Yeah, it is. It's messy and kind of illogical, but it happens. I can't honestly say that I know what you're going through, but I know you're hurting, and that it's blinding you to the obvious perk of all of this."

Bite your tongue, Griff . . .

She scoffs. "What perk could there possibly be?"

I flip onto my other side, reaching into the cooler to pull out her favorite top-shelf tequila and margarita mix. She gasps audibly.

Oh, thank God. I wasn't sure if that joke would land the way I wanted it to.

"Well, this would be disgusting alone," I say, carefully examining the margarita mix.

"Gimme!" She squeals, reaching over my chest

to grab the tequila. Her hair brushes against my neck and shoulders, and the scent of her shampoo washes over me.

God, she smells good.

"I can drink to that," she says, wrapping her pink lips around the mouth of the bottle and taking a swig of straight tequila.

"Fuck yeah, Anderson," I say, swiping the bottle from her to take a drag of poison myself. I shake off the initial burn.

It's time to get in the water. I do that *jump up to your feet without using your hands* trick, turning to Layne to pull her up with me. Her face is bright with laughter as she stares at me with an expression I can only call awe.

"What?" I ask.

"I don't think I've seen anyone besides my brother do that, and it was twenty years ago."

"What are you trying to say?" I straddle her with my legs, bending down until we're eye level. "You think I'm super cool?"

"I think you're super cute," she says with that charming half smile that says *don't try anything funny.* But her eyes are fixed squarely on my lips.

Interesting.

"Hmm, okay . . ." I pretend to contemplate that for a moment. "Would you think it's *cute* if I picked you up and threw you in that water over there?" I point to the ocean for effect.

She visibly shrinks back. "No, I wouldn't."

"Noted."

I back away with my hands lifted in surrender, giving her some space. Then, as if I were asking her to dance, I bow before her. "Lady Layne, would you do me the honor of joining me?"

"You're an idiot," she says with a chuckle, but it does the trick. Layne takes my hand and lets me lead her to the water. Her palm stays pressed against mine all the way to the edge, squeezing me tighter as the icy surf laps against her toes.

I make some lame joke about swimming through large bodies of tequila . . . just to get her laughing again. The low rumble of her laugh is addictive, and if I'm being honest, healing. I haven't felt this at ease in a long time. When she lets go of my hand, I feel the loss echo through my whole body.

Later, when the sun begins to set, I decide it's time to build the fire. It takes me a few minutes to carry the wood I brought in the car to our spot on the beach. Layne offers to help, but I can handle it. Instead, she puts herself to work setting up the tent. It's a simple one, the box promised a three-minute setup, so I decide to let her tackle it alone. By my fourth and final trip back from the car, she's securing the last of the ties. She looks over her shoulder at me, smug.

We make a good team.

As I stack up the extra logs beside the firepit, Layne sits down on a blanket and watches me, munching on the grapes and celery sticks left over from our lunch.

"What?" I ask.

"What do you mean, what?" she mumbles, her mouth full of celery.

"Do you have something to say to me?"

"No, why?" Her brow crinkles.

"Well, there's a beautiful sunset to your left, but you're too busy watching me manhandle my wood to notice." I grin at her discomfort, practically able to feel the heat of her cheeks from here.

In typical Layne fashion, she ignores my sexual innuendo and barrels into her argument. "I have yet to see any fire. I'm not convinced I won't be shivering in the darkness for the rest of the night."

There's the lawyer, always equipped with snark and double negatives.

Two can play at that game, sweetheart.

"I can think of other ways to keep warm."

When her mouth snaps shut, I think, *Did I take it too far? I'd better reel it in.*

"Don't worry. I was a Boy Scout for a short time. I remember how to make a fire. Or, at least, I remembered to bring lighter fluid," I say, splashing said fluid on the woodpile with fervor.

"Oh my God, Griffin. That's a lot."

"Oh, it's fine." I strike a match against the matchbox.

"Are you s—"

The flames roar to life with an audible *whoosh* when I drop the match in the center of the pile. Heat rolls off the wood like the waves of the near-by ocean, instantly enveloping us in warmth. I rub my hands together over my creation, admiring it. *That's a damn good fire.*

"You seem proud of yourself," Layne says, scooting closer to the fire. Closer to me.

"Not all of us are fancy career women. The rest of us little people have to make do with smaller accomplishments." I gesture at the flames, and in my best caveman voice, I growl, "Man make fire. Man feel good."

Layne snickers, bumping me with her elbow. I take a chance and wrap my arm around her, pulling her against my shoulder. She folds into me, easily resting her head against my chest. We stare at the flames, lost in the beauty of the moment.

A rush of relief washes over me. I feel calm. At peace.

And then my stomach growls.

"Is someone revving up their Jet Ski in the distance, or was that your stomach?" she asks, looking at me with big, sparkling eyes.

"Oh, now she has jokes," I say with a chuckle.

I reluctantly extract myself from her to set up the fireplace grill. Now, *this* I haven't done before. I bought this on a whim as I was picking up food and drinks for the day. Lucky for me, it's just a matter of adjusting the length of the legs to match the fire . . . which in my case, is aggressively high.

"Is it still *fine*?" she asks, quoting me from earlier.

"You bet," I say, my confidence unwavering.

With a spritz of margarita mix, I bring the fire down to a low, blue-white flame, and set the grill over it. One by one, I lay out rosemary-infused burger patties, long strips of red and green peppers, and two halves of corn on the cob. The smell is incredible.

"Okay, now *I'm* hungry," Layne says over my shoulder.

Within twenty minutes, we're both moaning into piping-hot burgers and talking through mouthfuls of watermelon-and-feta salad. The fact that this woman is gorgeous even when she's double-fisting a margarita and a corn cob proves there's something wrong with me. But I love how comfortable and safe she feels around me. She's not sucking her stomach in or worrying about the spot of ketchup on her cheek. She's just unapologetically herself.

But she's also a little different. She doesn't pull back when I use my thumb to wipe the ketchup off her cheek, nor does she seem to mind my staring. Is it the tequila?

Or is it something else?

As we clean up the carnage of our dinner, I repeatedly remind myself not to get my hopes up again. Every time I feel like I've gotten close to

Layne, she's pushed me away. After tonight, she'll probably shut me out for another six months.

I clench my jaw. *How much longer can I keep up with the whiplash?*

"I think I'm about ready to turn in," she says with a yawn.

The beach cover-up she threw on before we settled by the fire slips off one shoulder, and I swallow. *I want her.* I can't afford to waste time thinking about the off chance that Layne shuts me out again. She's let me back in for this moment, and I'll be damned if I don't make it count.

"I'll meet you in there," I murmur, reaching out to tuck a stray hair behind her ear.

Again, she doesn't back away. Instead, she just smiles, meets my eyes, and leans into my touch. I don't have time to process the moment, because as soon as it begins, it ends. The flap of the tent closes behind her with a quiet slide of fabric.

For a second, I watch Layne's silhouette as she ties her hair up, getting ready for bed. Then I turn back to the fire, dump the remains of a bottle of water on top, and wait for it to fizzle out.

When I step into the tent, Layne is propped up against a stack of pillows, dressed only in an oversized T-shirt from her college's alma mater. She isn't inside her sleeping bag. Instead, she's lying on top of it with a thin sheet over her. Her bare legs tangle in the sheet, exposing more skin than covering it. As her gaze locks with mine, her eyes soften.

I pull off my shirt, my eyes never leaving her. "This okay? I normally sleep in boxers or shorts."

She nods, still watching me. "Whatever you normally sleep in is fine." Her voice is lower than usual, almost husky.

With my heart beating out of my chest, I grab a pair of black athletic shorts from the top of my duffel bag and unlace my swim trunks. Layne's gaze wanders lower, caressing my chest and abs, then settle at where my hands have now paused in their work.

I turn and face the wall of the tent before dropping my swim trunks and stepping into my shorts. Feeling the heat of her gaze on my ass, I have to take a deep breath to calm myself down, because popping wood in these thin shorts isn't going to go unnoticed.

My sleeping bag is only a few inches from hers, and when I lie down on it, we're almost close enough to touch. Layne's chest rises and falls with a sigh. Her tongue darts out to wet her lips.

Is she nervous?

Once again, I lift my hand and tuck a strand of hair behind her ear. "I had fun with you today," I say softly.

She tilts her head, watching me. "Thanks for this. It was exactly what I needed to get out of my own head."

I'm about to make a joke about vitamin D solving all problems when she shifts closer and gives me *the look*. The look that says she wants me to kiss her. Her eyes flutter closed, and she wets her lower lip with her tongue.

Without any more prompting, I close the space between us, bringing my lips to hers in a gentle, chaste kiss. Her hands roam up my arms, ghosting over my biceps, my shoulders, before settling into my hair. She pulls me closer with a soft whimper. My fingers slide along her jawline, tilting her head slightly. Layne opens her mouth to me and her lips part, allowing me to deepen the kiss.

The second her tongue touches mine, my cock hardens. I taste watermelon and tequila, sweet and salty.

Layne gasps between kisses, but I won't stop to let her catch her breath. My dick is throbbing against the mesh of my shorts, begging to be touched. I moan into the kiss, my hand leaves her jaw to trail down her neck to her collarbone. My thumb brushes the top of her breast, and her back arches in approval. Kissing her slowly, deeply, I take her soft breast in my hand, reveling in the satisfaction of all my fantasies today. When I roll her nipple between my fingers through the thin material of her T-shirt, she jolts.

"Griff," she says softly, her voice filled with desire.

I let out a slow exhale, my heart pounding out an uneven rhythm. *This is finally going to happen.*

Her hands tease over the muscles in my chest, and she urges me closer. I roll on top of her, caging her in beneath me while I settle on my forearms. Our mouths break apart for a moment, and I gaze down at her heavy-lidded eyes.

"You're beautiful. You know that?"

Her lips tilt into a smile. "And you're a really good kisser." Crossing her ankles behind my back, Layne shifts, rocking us closer—until the heavy weight of my erection is pressed right between her legs. "Fuck . . ."

I press closer, angling my hips to rub my hard length over her sweet spot, and her lips part on a groan. "Yeah, sweetheart? That feel good?"

"Uh-huh." She moans, lost to the sensation.

I love that it's *me* making her feel good, and my head swims with that knowledge.

She's so warm beneath the cotton of her panties, I want to peel them back, touch her, and make her come on my fingers. But it's hard to pull myself away from her mouth, so I settle for dry-humping the shit out of her as we grind together. Mature, I know.

She's getting close. Her breathing has changed, grown more ragged, and her pulse thrums frantically in her neck. But I sense she's waiting for something.

"I want you to come," I murmur, sucking on the tender skin at the base of her throat.

A tremor rocks through her body, but then she pulls back. "Hold on. Wait," she says, her voice strained.

"What's wrong?"

Layne sits up and rakes a hand through her hair. "I can't do this."

Fuck. I sit up, trying to meet her eyes, but she stares straight ahead into the darkness.

"Look at me," I say, and she does, but I can't

read her expression. "Do you not want to?" Three seconds ago, I was pretty damn sure we were on the exact same page.

"I want to. But I won't," she says softly, shaking her head.

When was this decision made? And why wasn't I a part of it?

"You won't . . ."

"I won't use you to forget all of my problems. Sex would just be a temporary fix, and I don't want to ruin our friendship. You mean too much to me."

My brain struggles to comprehend what she's saying, which is difficult, given that all the blood in my body has rushed south.

"I would only be using you to relieve some stress," she says, finishing on an exhale.

"Ask me how many fucks I give." *Zero. The answer is zero.*

"Griffin." She says my name again, but this time, there's a slight edge to her voice. A warning.

"I'm serious. Use me. Ride off all that stress you've been under. Seriously, I volunteer as tribute."

She shakes her head with a wry smile.

"I want you to use me. Any which way you want." *I want you, Layne.*

"You say that now, but . . . I can't." And just like that, Layne lies back down, staring up at the ceiling of the tent.

I do the same, putting at least a foot of distance between us. At this point, I'm shaking with pent-up sexual need, but Layne doesn't owe me anything, and she doesn't have to explain herself. If she doesn't want this—then she doesn't, and maybe it's finally time for me to stop pining over her.

"I'm sorry," she whispers, her voice tight.

Dammit, Griffin. You brought her here to make her feel better, not worse. This wasn't supposed to be about sex.

On an exhale, I adjust my straining cock, tucking it beneath the waistband of my shorts and Layne doesn't fail to notice.

"Sorry, Griff," she murmurs, rolling onto her side to meet my eyes.

I turn to face her. "You have nothing to be sorry for."

She swallows, gaze moving down my torso before meeting my eyes once again. "It's just ... I couldn't live with myself if I ever used you for sex."

Use me, baby. Anytime you want. That's the first thought that flashes through my brain. Thankfully something more articulate comes out of my mouth. "No one's using anyone." I reach out to touch her cheek, my thumb caressing her soft skin. "Let me show you how desirable you are."

She chews on her lower lip and moves closer so slowly that I'm sure she's about to change her mind. She's as timid as a gazelle walking into a lion's den. But then she gathers her breath, and with it, her courage.

Her knees part and since her t-shirt has ridden up, I can see her panties and the damp spot in the fabric we put there.

Fuck. This is torture.

I touch her knee, and when her lips part on a shaky exhale, I slid my hand up, caressing the smooth skin of her inner thigh.

I lean in to kiss her and brush my fingers over her panties, touching her clit through the cotton barrier.

Her answering moan is the best sound. Soft and lovely.

She wants this as much as I do.

"Touch your pussy for me, Layne." I can't risk her slamming on the breaks again. This is going to move at her pace—whatever that is.

She gives me a look of hesitation, but behind it, there's heat too.

"Touch yourself," I murmur again.

Layne bites her lower lip, and my body tightens everywhere. And when her hand moves lower, down her body, I watch with rapt attention.

She doesn't pull the fabric to the side, but she slips her hand inside her panties and rubs in small circles. A needy whimper falls from her full mouth.

"That's it," I encourage as her hips move restlessly against her sleeping bag.

My heartrate skitters out of control like a train rumbling down the track, and I hold in a groan at the sight of her.

Watching Layne work herself toward release is the hottest thing I've ever seen. I touch her chin, tilting her mouth toward mine and the second her tongue touches mine, she starts to come—her entire body tightening and shaking as her orgasm crashes through her.

My heart riots against my ribs as hot lust pulses through me, settling low in my groin. The second

Layne pulls her damp fingers from her panties, I capture her wrist, drawing them into my mouth, tasting her sweet arousal.

My cock jolts as Layne makes a small noise of surprise.

"You taste so good." I press one last kiss to her fingers and then release her hand.

"What about you?" she breathes.

"What about me?" I'm going to die of a massive case of blue balls—no big deal.

She bites down on that full bottom lip again, conjuring up all kinds of dirty images in my head involving her mouth and my cock. "You can jerk it if you need to," she whispers.

My heart stops beating as her gaze tracks hotly down toward my erection. Without my permission, my right hand slips down my abs and under the elastic of my shorts. I don't draw my length out, I just curl my fist around my rigid shaft and stroke, my bicep flexing with the effort. A deep groan pours out of me.

Layne swallows heavily, her eyes glued to the spot where my hand moves in long measured strokes.

It feels so fucking good—mostly because of

the heated way she's watching me. And two minutes later, I'm coming all over my hand and stomach. Layne lifts up on her elbow, and brings her mouth to mine, kissing me deeply as the pleasure rocks through me.

After I'm cleaned up and dressed in a new pair of shorts, I curl onto my side and gather Layne in close. She wouldn't let me touch her tonight, but she doesn't stop me from holding her. It's something, I guess. I close my eyes, feeling pretty damn certain that sleep will be impossible tonight.

ELEVEN

Layne

Present day

As I walk into the small, cozy waiting room, the glowing aromatherapy machine in the corner puffs a stream of vapor out into the air. I can't quite place the smell—something herbal and soothing with a little lavender in it, maybe—but it instantly puts my mind a little more at ease as I sit on the edge of one of the overstuffed armchairs along the perimeter of the room. A large painting of a sunset over the ocean hangs on the wall across from me, and I zone out, staring at the sweeping strokes of red and orange that fade into subtle pinks and yellows.

It's only my fourth session with my new therapist, but I have to say, it feels like it's working.

Whatever that means in this context. Sure, I'm still stressed and unsure about my life, but so far, just having someone else to dump all my anxieties on has made my future feel a little more manageable.

Plus, I'm absolutely obsessed with how warm and comforting Dr. Benson's whole office is, from the Himalayan salt lamp on a side table near the door, to the plush cream-colored couch, to the soothing artwork on the walls. It's like everything is designed to make you feel at ease—which, come to think of it, it probably is.

The door to Dr. Benson's office opens, and the sweet older lady pops her head out, her silver chin-length hair hanging loosely around her gently lined face, her tortoise-shell horn-rimmed glasses perched on the bridge of her nose.

"Hi, Layne. It's good to see you. Come on in."

Adjusting my purse strap over my shoulder, I walk into her office, settling myself onto the couch as she takes her usual seat in the armchair across from me and reaches for the small notepad next to her.

"So, how are you doing today?" she asks with a smile, the lines around her mouth deepening.

"Oh, you know, I'm fine. Just the usual," I say with a soft chuckle, crossing one leg over the other.

I'm still not sure why I insist on playing this game every week—the one where I say I'm fine and she presses me for more details. But after thirty-seven years of pretending everything's fine, I'm not quite ready yet to spill my guts immediately upon seeing someone. Even if that someone is my therapist.

"Mm-hmm. And tell me more about *the usual*." Dr. Benson cocks her head to the side, her pale blue eyes on mine.

I stare at her for a moment before sighing and pushing my fingers through my hair. "Well, things at work are as stressful as ever. I tried some of the prioritizing techniques you recommended last week, and they helped a little, but I still feel like I can't quite get a handle on everything."

She nods along as I speak, scribbling away on her notepad. "Okay, so you're still struggling to feel in control at work. Is anything else bothering you? *The usual* sounds . . . ominous." She smiles gently.

"I mean, there's also the whole *thirty-seven and still single as fuck* thing. Sorry for cursing," I quickly add, lowering my gaze to the carpet. *Classy, Anderson.*

"You don't need to apologize. Swear words can

help us relieve stress. If letting out a hearty *fuck* now and then makes you feel better, then by all means, let it out."

I can't help but giggle, my eyebrows shooting straight up to my hairline. Never in my life did I think I'd hear my sixty-five-year-old therapist say the phrase "hearty fuck," let alone encourage me to use it too.

"All righty then, I'll keep that in mind." I grin at her.

"Where do you think your anxiety about being single at your age comes from?" she asks after a slight pause, her eyes trained on the notepad as she finishes whatever it is she's writing.

"Oh, I don't know. I guess I just always thought I'd be settled down with kids by now. Ever since I can remember, I've wanted a family of my own. And now I'm at that age, where every day that passes and I'm still single, the further and further away I get from making that dream a reality."

"Have you considered raising a child on your own? Plenty of women your age do. There's not nearly the same stigma about it as there once was."

"Being a single mom was never something I wanted for myself. I can barely manage my work-life balance as it is. Besides, I already bought my dream home for myself instead of waiting around for Mr. Right. Don't get me wrong, my house is amazing, and I don't regret buying it for a second. But being in that space alone, no matter how perfect it might be, can make bad days worse sometimes, you know?"

"Mmm. And are you taking any steps to find someone?"

I snort. "Uh, taking steps feels like an understatement."

Dr. Benson simply raises her eyebrows, prompting me to continue.

"I spend at least two hours a day reexamining what I'm looking for in a man. Practically every successful man over forty I meet, I see as a prospect, and do my best to win over while simultaneously slipping in casual-sounding questions about whether they're single or if they want kids. I tried online dating for a while, but after too many awkward, stilted dates to count, I gave up on that front too. Although I did just hear about a new website that matches high-achieving singles over thirty-five, which, if I'm being honest, sounds depressing as hell. But, hey, I'm not in a position to be picky. I don't know, I guess I'm just starting to think that I'm doomed to end up alone. Forever."

Dr. Benson stares at me, her eyes wide and watching my face carefully, no longer glued to her notepad. She doesn't say anything for a few beats, letting the weight of what I just shared hang in the air between us. "Is that all?" she finally asks, the sarcasm in her voice hard to miss.

"I know it sounds like a lot, but I don't know what else to do."

"How about having a little fun?"

"What do you mean?"

Dr. Benson smiles softly, setting her notepad to the side and leaning forward to rest her elbows on her knees. "Layne, it's clear that finding a good match is very important to you. But I think that in taking your search so seriously, you've somehow managed to suck every ounce of fun out of dating."

I look away, staring instead at the motivational poster on the wall of a turtle climbing up a hill, totally at a loss for how to respond. "I have fun," I murmur defensively, crossing one leg over the other.

"When's the last time you let loose? It sounds like you spend all day micromanaging every aspect of your life. Do you leave any room for the unexpected?"

"Well, I'd argue that every man I date who turns out to be a dud or an asshole is unexpected."

"That may be," she replies, leaning back in her chair and giving me a knowing look. "But all I'm saying is that it might do you some good to remember what it's like to enjoy yourself again. All work and no play is a recipe for loneliness and depression, no matter how good you are at your job."

Nodding slowly, I keep staring at the damn turtle poster on the wall, pressing my lips together as tears sting the corners of my eyes. *Dammit, I hate it when she's right.*

"I don't see how *having fun* is going to make anything better. It just seems like a waste of time at this point."

"It might not always feel like it, but you're still young, with plenty of life ahead of you. Take it from me. Switching up your routine might be good for you. You never know what's out there until you stop looking for it."

With Dr. Benson's parting words ringing in my head, we say our good-byes and I gather my things, my mind spinning during the whole drive home. It's not like she's never given me direct advice before, but damn, you know your life is depressing when your sixty-five-year-old therapist tells you to go out and get laid.

Okay, maybe she didn't say anything about getting laid. But, let's be real. It was implied.

When I get home, I flop down on the couch, racking my brain for something fun and unexpected that I could do tonight. The clubs I used to frequent in my twenties are out of the question. I highly doubt I'll find my soul mate in the middle of a neon-lit dance floor, trying to escape the sweaty, unsolicited bodies rubbing up against my backside. The mere thought of it sends grossed-out chills down my spine.

For as much anxiety as my age gives me, I'm definitely glad to not be in that phase of my life anymore. Then again, here I am, trying to decide what bar to hit up and which outfit will best accentuate my curves while still holding everything in.

As if on cue, my phone buzzes, and I pick it up to find a text from Kristen, inviting me to drinks with the crew tonight. Well, inviting isn't quite the right word. More like demanding.

For a second, I wonder if she's working for Dr. Benson. The timing is just too perfect.

But before I can let myself go down *that* paranoid rabbit hole, I force myself to shake it off. It's one thing to be single at my age. If I start suspecting that everyone trying to help me is out to get me, it's a slippery slope to adopting twenty cats and never leaving my home again.

I shoot her a quick text letting her know that I'll be there. She responds with a bunch of excited emojis, and I can practically hear her squealing with delight.

It's not like I turn down *all* of her invitations to go out with our friends but it has been a while since I've had a fun night out. And that definitely includes going home with some rando from the bar.

With only a couple of hours before I need to leave, I figure I'd better start getting ready now. I used to love this part of going out, the hours spent primping and priming, making yourself as smooth and pretty as possible before going out for the night. Now, with my goals a bit more focused than they used to be, I'm inclined to take a more clinical approach to the whole process, optimizing the way I look and smell so I'm as desirable as possible without looking like a *total* one-night stand. I'm looking for a bit more longevity now that I'm no longer in my twenties.

This new process includes a lot of the same things as before—washing my body with a lightly scented bodywash, shaving practically every surface of my skin, exfoliating, using my best moisturizer, putting on my good underwear, blow-drying my hair and curling it into loose waves, and applying a fresh, slightly less natural than usual face of makeup. Heck, I even decide to match my bra to my panties—and by that, I mean they're both black. I can't remember the last time I bought a matching set of lingerie.

After dabbing a soft pink shade of lipstick onto my lips, I take a step back from the full-length mirror to take it all in.

I went with a knee-length, formfitting maroon dress I haven't worn in years, which, honestly, fits way better than I remember. The fabric is tight and thick enough that I don't feel like I need to wear any shapewear underneath, thank God. I'm all for the miracle of Spanx, but it's nice to be able to breathe too.

Stepping into a pair of strappy black heels, I call an Uber, checking my texts to make sure Kristen hasn't yelled at me for being late yet. Thankfully, she's running a little late too, but she assures me that the group is already there.

I check my reflection one last time before walking out the door, silently pleased with how my dark waves fall around my cleavage—and how my ass looks in this dress, if I'm being honest. If I were a guy, I'd want to take the girl in the mirror home.

She looks confident, refined, and sexy as hell. A sly smile sneaks across my lips as my phone dings, letting me know the Uber driver is here.

I give the girl in the mirror a wink before walking out the door. Who knows, maybe tonight is the night she'll meet someone. Someone who'll make her feel as sexy and desirable and worthy of her dreams as she wants to be.

After all, it's doctor's orders.

TWELVE

Griffin

This bar is noisy as hell, but I can't say that's a bad thing. I have to lean down so Layne's lips are brushing against my ear, just so I can hear her. And, *fuck*, if that isn't fuel for every fantasy I keep returning to . . . you know the one. Of our naked bodies, finally entwined.

"You should really do therapy," she yells before pulling another sip from the straw in her tequila sunrise.

Kristin and her new boyfriend are leaning over the bar, ordering their next round of drinks, while Layne and I kill some time at the old-fashioned jukebox. I lean against the metal and plastic along the side, browsing the songs for an oldie but goodie.

"What?" I ask, pretending not to hear her.

"You heard me," she yells again.

The feel of her hot breath on my neck sends chills down my spine, straight to the growing tightness in my jeans. I close the space between us, so our faces are only inches apart. Her eyelids flutter at the proximity, and I meet her gaze with a smirk. I know I affect her, even if she pretends I don't. Layne tries to pretend it didn't, but something changed between us after that camping trip. It's little things, like the way her gaze lingers on me too long, or how she pretends not to be affected when we're standing close like this.

"What do you want to listen to?" I ask, tapping on the glass of the jukebox.

"You're deflecting," she says, but still leans over my arm to look at her options.

My fingers flex across the glass involuntarily as the fabric of her tight red dress brushes against my arm. "I like your dress. Did you learn that word from your therapist?" I ask her, my gaze wandering across her body.

Damn, dude. At least try to hide how hungry you are.

"No," she says, turning to me with a laugh.

"I know what deflecting means, thank you very much." Her dark curls hang loosely on her shoulders, framing her breasts.

Impossibly, I drag my gaze up to hers. "Red is definitely your color."

"It's maroon, and I know." She smiles at me shyly. Pulling at her purse, she removes a handful of quarters from its depths and slides them one by one into the coin slot.

I mentally kick myself for not paying for it myself. For being too busy soaking up how close we're standing, how good she smells, how gracefully she moves . . .

"I felt inspired," she says as she slides the last quarter into the machine, then pushes the buttons to make her selections.

"Because of therapy?" I ask.

"It was either wear the red dress, or accept my fate as a cat lady."

"You don't have any cats," I say with a laugh.

"Not yet," she says, pointing with a polished nail to punctuate her point.

I open my mouth to continue this dance that we're so familiar with . . . the playful banter, the harmless flirting. But I press my lips together when the song starts playing over the speakers.

"I love this song." She sighs happily as "Dancing in the Moonlight" by King Harvest covers us like a soft rain. Her face lights up as she begins singing along to the words of the first verse.

A grin stretches across my face as I watch Layne move to the music, her hands planted on either side of the jukebox, her hips swaying with the upbeat rhythm. On a whim, I take her hand, twirling her around and drawing her into me. We don't miss a beat.

"It looked like you needed a better dance partner," I say.

Layne beams up at me, her inhibitions lowered, thanks to the help of a little liquid courage and a classic bop. We rock together, either unaware or uncaring that no one else in this crowded bar is dancing.

"Everybody's feeling warm and bright . . ."

As I sing into her ear, she shudders pleasantly against me. Her hand slides from my bicep up onto my shoulder, firmly planting on the back of my neck. Her thumb caresses my nape, and my system floods with warmth and comfort.

She must be feeling this too. Right?

Layne rests her forehead against my shoulder and sighs. I adjust, lifting her chin so that our eyes meet with a look that asks *what's wrong?*

She smiles, almost sadly. My lips turn down in concern, and she shakes her head.

"I just need some air," she yells over the music.

My brow furrows. *What just happened?*

Layne detaches herself from me and makes her way to the exit. I want to follow her, but don't know if she wants me to.

As she disappears through the doors, I do a quick scan of the crowd, looking for my sister. Sure enough, there she is, wrapped in the arms of her new guy, chatting with another couple at the bar. I pull my phone out and shoot her a quick text to let her know that Layne and I are grabbing some air.

I make my way through the throngs of people, reaching the door only moments after Layne. The night breeze wafts over my face and arms, relieving me of that stuffy, sticky bar feeling.

Layne leans against the brick wall of the neighboring furniture shop, absently scrolling through her phone. I pull my phone out again and shoot her a text.

```
You okay? I'm here if you wanna
talk.
```

Layne reads the message, then looks over to the door where I'm standing. She sighs again, this time not in a sad way . . . in a different way. She beckons me to her with a nod of her head.

"Sorry for walking out like that," she says as I approach her.

There's something terribly fragile about this moment, like the air around us is wavering, and the light cast down from the streetlight is buzzing with something important to say.

I don't know what's happening, but I know I have to be careful. "It was hot in there, anyway. Have I told you how great you look?"

Layne throws her head back with a hearty laugh, stealing a smile from me. "Yes," she says with a chuckle. "You did mention that. A few times."

"I mean, I had to. I look like a total frat boy next to you," I say, pulling at my vintage print tee with mock disgust.

"Hardly." Her eyes narrow at me again, but her face still glows with that gorgeous smile. "The only difference is that I tried extra hard to look nice tonight, and you didn't."

This body needs no extra effort, I almost joke. This isn't the time for jokes, though. If I've learned anything from being with Layne, it's to read a room. Or, in this case, a street corner.

I lean against the wall next to her, our bare arms only separated by a few inches of cold brick. "What made you try extra hard tonight?"

I have a gut feeling that it's something to do with her therapy session earlier today. It's fresh in her mind, considering she brought it up while we were inside. Layne isn't exactly an open book, or at least she isn't the kind of person to bring up her mental health so flippantly in the middle of a bar. Something's obviously eating at her.

"I just wanted to put myself out there tonight. Try and *have some fun* or something," she says, air quotes and all. She shakes her head with an empty laugh. "I'm just so unmotivated."

"Why's that?" I look down at her, unable to see her eyes anymore, just those lush dark lashes.

"Because . . . well, all I want to do is hang out with you."

My heart leaps. *Okay . . . I didn't see that coming.*

"So, let me get this straight," I say after a few

moments of weighted silence. "You want to meet someone tonight, put this dress to work . . . but you only want to be with me."

Layne turns away with a shrug, her expression unreadable. "I know, it's silly. It's just so easy to be with you, and so hard to . . . always be on the lookout."

"Okay," I say, flipping a mental coin. *Heads, I take the safe route. Tails, I go for it.*

Who am I kidding? It was always going to be tails.

"I think I have a solution for that," I say, nudging her with my elbow.

She rocks slightly on her heels with a giggle, meeting my eyes with an uncharacteristically shy look. "What?"

I step forward and position my body directly in front of hers. If I raised my arms and placed my hands on the cold brick, I could lock her against my body and . . .

Patience, Griff. You've come this far.

"You could work on both of those goals tonight, you know?"

"How?" She sounds slightly breathless.

"Come home with me."

Layne stares at me in a way she hasn't ever before. Several silent seconds tick past, and I'm sure she's going to shoot me down. Just like she has every other time.

"Okay." Her voice is soft, barely above a whisper, but her gaze is hot on mine.

Wait, what?

I blink, and my mouth hangs open. Finally, I ask, "Okay?"

"Yeah.."

I squeeze my eyes closed and then reopen them, testing the reality of this situation. Layne watches me with something like amusement woven into her smile.

Yep, still real, still happening.

"Okay, I'll get a car," I say, pulling out my phone.

I remember to text my sister and send her a brief, perhaps cryptic message. Something about a migraine and calling it a night. By the looks of it, she'll be too preoccupied with being in love to spare a second thought for my whereabouts.

"One thing," Layne says, and my heart braces

for impact. "We're going to my place."

My dick throbs painfully against the zipper of my jeans, and my mouth lifts in a smile. Layne in charge is the hottest Layne.

It's a quick eight-minute drive from the bar to Layne's house . . . some stroke of luck. Is God rewarding me for my year of celibacy? Did some higher power finally decide to throw me a bone?

Speaking of which, the appendage trying to pound through my jeans is actually painful enough that I have to discreetly adjust it while Layne talks to the driver. I feel like I'm lost in a dream when I step out of the car, following the sway of Layne's hips as she leads me up the stairs of her porch.

Inside, the lights are off, and I can hear the distant hum of the dishwasher. Immediately, I'm comfortable and at ease. I love this house, and I rarely get to see it these days. Everything has its rightful place . . . from the modest drink cart to the faux alpaca rug sprawled in front of the fireplace. I don't waste much time admiring her living arrangement, however. The soft sound of Layne's voice snaps my attention back to her as she stands at the end of the hall.

"Do you need anything? Water? A beer?" she asks, her heels hanging in one hand as the other rests lightly on the door frame of her dimly lit bedroom. Her silhouette strikes me as heavenly, all curves and natural grace.

I lick my lips. "No, I don't need anything."

"Then get in here," she says, stepping into her room and dropping her heels on the soft shag rug just inside.

I follow her inside as if in a trance. Layne stands with her back to me, unzipping the back of her dress, almost urgently. I catch her hands before she gets it free.

"Let me," I murmur, brushing my fingertips against the soft skin of one exposed shoulder blade.

Faint chill bumps rise on her back as she shivers from my touch, and I'm suddenly thrust back into the memory of our first meeting, that fateful day in her office when my hands touched her back for the first time.

I press my body against hers, my erection nestled firmly against her backside. As I slowly draw the zipper of the maroon dress down, Layne melts into me. Her hands find my thighs and squeeze, *hard*, as I press the softest kisses onto one slim shoulder. She tastes sweet and practically melts into my touch.

Once the zipper is low enough, I kneel behind her, pulling the fabric down with me until it pools around her bare feet. I run my hands from the dip in her lower back to her sexy little thong, loving the way her soft skin feels beneath my fingertips.

Layne turns around, gazing down on me with hooded eyes. Her fingers brush over my shoulders, trailing up to dig fingernails deliciously into my scalp. I plant open-mouthed kisses against her hips and waist, nipping at the sensitive flesh above the line of her underwear.

"Griffin," she says on a moan.

It's too much to hear my name on those lips, like *that*. I rise to my feet and cup her face in my hands, fitting my mouth against hers. Our kiss is slow, hot, and wet, like water finally brought to a boil. *Jesus.* I can feel all the pent-up sexual tension that we've been stockpiling for years, echoing between our buzzing bodies.

Gently, I change the angle of our kiss, deepening it with a soft push of my tongue against hers. Layne presses tightly against me, her half-naked body hot against my clothes.

"Take off your shirt," she gasps between kisses.

"Anything for you," I murmur, ripping it over my head with one swift motion.

I draw Layne back against me, our bare skin lighting a fire between us. Her hands massage the exposed muscles of my shoulders, and I moan into our kiss.

"Fuck, Layne . . ."

Step by step, she leads me to the side of her bed. She gently pulls me down with her, and I follow, greedy for the taste of her neck on my tongue. My hands find her breasts, squeezing gently at first, and then harder when she arches her back and grinds her pelvis into mine.

So, Layne likes it a little rough. I'd be lying if I said I wasn't taking notes.

But when she pants out, "Condom," my heart stops and my brain scrambles in sixteen different directions.

Fuck. This can't be happening.

"I don't have one. Do you?" I ask, praying to that higher power for just one more favor.

"No." She groans, and her hands fall from my back, bouncing against the mattress.

Is she pouting?

"We don't need a condom to have fun," I say before pulling the cup of her bra down to reveal one perfect pink nipple.

She yelps as I lick a wet path across her breast with my tongue. My fingers find the edge of her underwear, dipping beneath the fabric to discover even more silky skin.

"Can I take these off?" I murmur against her rising and falling belly.

She nods, making a desperate little sound that tells me, *yes, for God's sake, yes.*

Drawing myself up onto my knees, I pull her panties down her legs and am completely awe-struck. Layne is perfectly clean shaven, pink and wet. My mouth waters.

"You're so beautiful," I whisper, my breath tickling the skin of her inner thighs.

I lick and nip my way up her legs until I reach her beautiful, precious cunt. With soft, chaste kisses, I elicit needy whimpers from her.

Layne's fingernails drag almost painfully through my hair, telling me to make my move already. When I caress her with my tongue, Layne bucks against my mouth, so I hold her hips in place with my strong hands. I suck and lick and kiss her pussy until I feel her quivering with pleasure. Then I draw one finger into my mouth, making it warm and wet.

With my lips tight around her clit, I press in one thick finger, then two. Her inner walls throb and constrict, signaling her orgasm rolling in. With steady strokes of my tongue and rhythmic pumping of my fingers, I pull her orgasm out of her. Her body rocks against my mouth like she's riding a bull at the rodeo. I freaking love it.

A minute or two passes before she finally settles, the last waves of her orgasm lapping against her as I leave soft kisses on any surface I can reach. I crawl up her body, nestling into the crook of her neck with a sigh.

"Your turn," she whispers against my neck.

Layne gently pushes one of my shoulders until I lose my balance. Before I know it, I'm on my back, and she has her mouth on my skin, leaving languid kisses down my chest and abs. The palm of her hand finds purchase on my balls, and my hips thrust involuntarily.

"Fuck," I murmur with a hiss of breath.

She chuckles as she massages them in her hand, casually sending fireworks up my spine and straight back into my rock-hard dick. *I don't think I've ever been this worked up before.* I lift my upper body from the bed, finding her neck and shoulders with my hands. Layne meets my eyes, just as the tip of her tongue touches my cock. I shudder, overcome with the sensation of her soft kisses against my hardness.

She closes her eyes and opens her mouth, completely enveloping me in warmth and slickness, taking me fully and then sucking softly as she eases back. The second time she takes me, she meets my eyes. My head spins.

"You're so fucking sexy," I say, letting my head fall back on the bed. I can't keep watching her . . . I don't want to blow a load too quickly when it feels *this* good.

Because Layne is damn good with her mouth.

"Fuck, Layne," I murmur, and she hums in appreciation. The vibrations almost set me off right there. I take a handful of her hair, careful to only hold it back and not force a rhythm. This woman knows exactly what she's doing.

Layne speeds up, applying more suction and uses one hand to cup my balls.

God bless America. She's a multi-tasker.

I feel my orgasm coming, barreling toward me like it never has before. "Fuck, Layne—fuck. I'm going to—"

I groan out the words, giving her the chance to release her lip lock on my cock and finish me off neatly, with a simple hand job. But, no. She only takes me deeper into her throat, rubbing the vein of my cock with her tongue.

Stealing a glance at her beautiful face, her mouth so full of me, I can't hold back any longer. I come hard and long into Layne's hot throat, and she swallows me down with the ease of an experienced lover.

Fuck. I inhale sharply, exhaling in shaky bursts. My head is still spinning.

Did that actually happen?

Holy shit.

It did. And it was better than I could have ever imagined.

THIRTEEN

Layne

All those times I imagined what Griffin's body looks like through his T-shirt, based on the outline of his rippling abs, firm pecs, and defined biceps? Yeah, whatever I came up with doesn't hold a candle to what he actually looks like naked.

And I can't fucking believe I'm lying here naked next to him.

If someone had told me only six months ago that I'd be hooking up with my best friend's younger brother, I would have said they were dead wrong. If they'd told me I'd be hooking up with him and not worried about my jiggly ass or slight muffin top, I'd have said they were fucking insane. And yet here I am, climbing all over his ripped, absolutely perfect body, and the only thing on my mind is how natural this feels—and why the hell didn't we do this way sooner?

"What are you thinking about?" he asks, rolling over onto his side and brushing a stray hair from my cheek. His fingertips wander down my neck but his eyes stay on mine, and his soft touches send goose bumps racing down my spine.

"Nothing, really. I'm just happy," I say, propping myself up on my side to mirror him.

Without thinking, I move closer to him, our legs intertwining, our faces inches apart. Everything with him is instinctual, almost animalistic in how easy it is. Like our bodies know what to do, even if my mind might be a few steps behind.

"Me too."

Griffin's mouth meets mine in a long, slow, lingering kiss, one that sends shock waves straight to my core, lighting up every single nerve ending in my body.

Where the hell did he learn to kiss like this? For all the shit I used to give him about being a player, in this moment, I totally get it. If he has skills like this, then for the sake of all women everywhere, he needs to use them.

Lucky for me, right now he's *definitely* using

them.

"How are you so sexy?" Griffin murmurs, kissing my neck as my breath catches in my throat, all the blood in my head rushing to my center.

"How are . . . you so . . . good at this?" I ask, slightly breathless, but enjoying every touch of his lips to my skin.

He doesn't reply. Instead, he guides me onto my back and slips a hand between my legs, his fingers moving gently as though he's testing the limits, checking to see if I'm ready for more. For the record, I definitely am, even if I'm not sure I'll be able to have another orgasm after the way he devoured me.

"Griffin. Shit." I curse as his fingers find a perfect rhythm, and his lips trail over my neck and down one shoulder.

My hands grasp at his firm, muscular back, fighting for purchase. Any awareness of what I look like or even what my fucking name is fades away, leaving nothing but white-hot pleasure in its wake. With every move he makes, something swells inside me, and I can't help the moans and sighs that escape from deep within.

Just as I'm about to reach my peak, he pulls me on top of him without missing a beat. I'm about to protest until I realize this position has its advantages. My center aligns perfectly with his thick manhood, and I shamelessly grind myself all over him.

A deep groan vibrates in his throat as he watches me with a dark, hooded gaze.

His hands skim up my sides, and he palms the weight of my breasts, pinching one nipple. All at once, an orgasm crashes over me. Arching my spine so my hair falls back over my shoulders, I inhale sharply and plant my hands against his firm abs to ground myself.

Coming down from the natural high with a groan, I slide off of him and onto my side, my back to him. He chuckles into my shoulder—which somehow turns me on even more. Without saying a word, he spoons me in a way that makes me feel calm and safe and protected, his arms encircling my body as his hand explores the terrain.

We lie like that for a little while longer while my breathing slows.

"That was amazing," I say, breathless.

"We're just getting started," he whispers, one hand dipping between my legs while the other massages my breast. Pleasure riots through me, making my heart pound. He works his fingers over my needy center until my breath grows ragged and

I'm practically begging him to let me come again.

"Griff . . . please," I whisper, turning and crushing my mouth to his over my shoulder.

Reaching behind me, I take him in my hand, my fingers barely meeting around his shaft. He groans as I begin my mission of making him feel as good as he's making me.

"Fuck, that's so good," he murmurs, clearly enjoying himself, but his fingers don't waver for a second.

He pushes one thick finger inside me, and I shudder around him, doing my best to stay focused. He pushes in a second, and I yelp as he begins pumping, timing his movements with mine. With his free hand, he rolls my nipple between his thumb and forefinger, reducing me to a moaning, whimpering mess.

Griffin thrusts into my fist, his hot breath on my neck. There's sensation everywhere.

Suddenly, I can't take it—another orgasm rips through my center at the same time his erupts from him. Our bodies quake together as wave after wave of pleasure consumes us until we collapse onto the bed, chests heaving, beads of sweat dotting our foreheads.

We lie there in silence for a while. Our breathing evens out, and he tucks his arm under my head as I curl up next to him.

I haven't had sex like that since . . .

Who am I kidding? I've never had sex like that, let alone sex like that without penetration.

Sure, I've been with guys who were good in bed, but no one has ever come anywhere close to what just happened. I didn't just feel cherished . . . I felt fucking worshipped. No man has ever been so attentive to my needs before, so careful and controlled while still being totally wild.

Griffin shifts behind me and pulls a few tissues from a box beside the bed, and then I feel him wiping away the mess he made on my lower back and butt. When he's done, he tugs me close again.

A smile pulls at the corners of my mouth as I lift my chin to study his profile, a hint of a shadow of stubble perfectly defining his jaw. As if he could sense me watching him, he turns and looks at me, his blue-green eyes piercing mine.

"You were . . ." I pause, and a stupid smile spreads across my face while I try to find the right word.

"Incredible? Mind-blowing? Absolutely the

best you've ever had?" he says, the grin on his face matching mine.

"Oh, shut up. I was going to say decent," I tease, swatting his chest and fake rolling my eyes.

"Decent? You came three times. I think I earned more than *decent*."

His eyes dance like they only do when he's teasing me, and normally that would make my blood boil. But this time, my blood's boiling for an entirely different reason.

"Fine," I say, resting my chin on his chest. "You were good. Like, too good. Are you sure they weren't paying you to give your clients a little extra attention at that massage job?"

He chuckles, brushing his fingertips along my bare arm. "If that were the case, you would have been the first to know."

Happy chills run down my spine at the mention of the first time we met, before I knew he was Kristen's brother, before I even knew his last name.

That was when he was just some kid who asked me on a date, a piece of man candy I'd only let myself fantasize about late at night when I needed help falling asleep. Little did I know then what he'd come to mean to me—let alone the fact that he'd one day be naked in my bed.

Out of nowhere, my stomach grumbles loud enough for him to hear, and his eyebrows shoot up to his hairline, his eyes crinkling in amusement.

"Wait right here," he says, slipping out from under me and gently placing my head on a pillow.

"Where are you—"

But before I can finish my question, he's half-way down the hall, and all I can do is watch his tight ass at work while he walks away.

I sit up, half-aware of the fact that I'm still naked, and decide to take the moment of solitude to run to the bathroom. Wiping off some mascara smudges under my eyes, I can hear him rummaging around in my kitchen, the sound of cabinets opening and closing serving as the countdown clock to fix myself up a bit before he gets back.

Quickly sitting down on the toilet to pee, I run my fingers through my hair to get the knots out without totally flattening the *I just had three orgasms* volume I've already got going on.

After flushing the toilet, I wash my hands and study my reflection in the large, floor-to-ceiling mirror in front of me. With any other guy, I'd be fixing my makeup or applying a little lip gloss, but right now, I like the woman staring back at me. Sure, her hair's a little crazy and she's slightly flushed, but she looks happy, alive. Nothing like the woman I was only a few days ago.

At the sound of Griffin's footsteps in the hallway, I leave the bathroom and climb back into bed, propping myself up on my elbows and pulling my hair to one side. He walks in, his arms full of every box of snacks I have in this house—which, if I'm being honest, isn't much. But just seeing the proud look on his face as he stands there, his tall, lean frame filling the doorway, is enough to rouse my appetite.

"I've hunted. I've gathered. And now I've returned," he says, delicately placing his findings at the foot of the bed, which include a half-eaten bag of low-calorie kettle corn, two boxes of whole wheat and flaxseed crackers, and an unopened package of chocolate chip cookies I'd been saving for *that* time of the month.

"My hero," I say, and honestly, I'm half-serious. My stomach growled earlier for a reason. Grabbing the kettle corn, I help myself to a handful.

"You have the worst snacks I've ever seen in my entire life," he says, sitting next to me and examining the back of a box of crackers.

"I try not to keep too much snack food in the house," I reply between handfuls of popcorn.

"I can see why." His mouth twitches up into a smile as he gives me a sidelong glance, but I just swat at his arm with the back of my hand. "Don't worry. I like a woman with an appetite."

I roll my eyes, but on the inside, I'm sighing in relief. I haven't thought about it before this moment, but I've totally let my guard down around him in a way I've never done before. Not only have I been completely butt naked around a man who spends at least six days a week at the gym, I'm now scarfing down snack food in front of him. Sure, I take care of myself, but I definitely don't spend as much time on my body as he does. And honestly? This whole night has felt like the most natural thing in the world.

"So, are you going to share any of that, or should I just hunker down with these flaxseed crackers?"

I laugh, throwing a couple of pieces of popcorn at him, totally missing his mouth and hitting his chest and forehead instead.

"Oh, it's on," he says, lunging for the popcorn as I pull it away, starting a whole new game of cat and mouse.

It's silly, but I can't stop smiling. Laughing, the

two of us wrestle over the popcorn and cookies and end up tangled up in each other's limbs. We spend the rest of the night talking and eating and kissing and cuddling.

And if I'm being honest with myself, I can't remember the last time a hookup was this fun.

FOURTEEN

Layne

After a long day at the office, and then a hot shower, I'm lying in bed at barely nine o'clock on a Tuesday night when my cell phone chimes from beside me.

I turn it over to find a text from Griffin.

Hey chica.

I smile and shake my head.

Hey stud. What's up?

Flirting with him this way is entirely new and unexpected and a big piece of me absolutely loves it. I guess some part of me really took my therapist's comments to heart. I'm definitely putting myself out there and having more fun. And while it won't lead to anything serious, she was right—it's surprisingly freeing to give in to temptation. Especially when that temptation is six feet of virile masculinity with a wide, firm chest and jaw-dropping good looks.

His reply comes seconds later.

I'm horny.

Those two little words are followed by a photo of his junk. His white boxer-clad junk, that looks halfway to erect, and a portion of his firm, chiseled abs.

A hot current of desire flashes through me.

Come over, I type out.

Yeah?

Yes, I write back.

His isn't the most romantic proposition, but after the last time he was here, I haven't stopped thinking about what we did right here in this very bed.

`Bring   condoms,` I add on hoping I don't sound like some desperate horny college co-ed.

Just as my mind is beginning to spin, wondering exactly how Griffin views me, he replies with a thumbs-up emoji and I dissolve into a fit of laughter.

Twenty minutes later, I've poured two glasses of wine and lowered the lights in my living room. But the moment Griffin lets himself in, the air around us changes. He crosses the room in three easy strides and then he's pulling me into his arms. When his mouth lowers to mine, I part my lips and tease his tongue with my own.

A rough groan escapes the back of his throat. "Missed you," he murmurs.

"Bedroom," I pant as his lips travel down my neck, stopping at my collarbone.

The wine sits forgotten on the coffee table and we make our way down the hall, unable to keep our hands to ourselves.

Once inside my room, Griffin stands in front of me, and lifts my chin toward his. His mouth covers mine in a hot, urgent kiss, his tongue moving in confident strokes until I'm practically squirming with desire.

When I drop to my knees on the floor in front of him, it's not some well-thought out plan, it's just need. I *need* my mouth on him. Need to touch and tease and taste him.

"Haven't been able to stop thinking about you," he admits as I lower his zipper and draw his thick cock from his jeans.

He caresses my hair and gazes down at me with an adoring expression as I welcome the first few inches of him into my mouth. I don't go slow, I'm so needy for him.

"Layne, *fuck*," he groans, burying his hand in my hair.

I can't resist bringing one hand between my legs to touch myself as I pleasure him, but when Griffin notices, he growls and pulls away, hauling me to my feet.

"Need to be inside you."

"Yes," I groan, body already clenching with anticipation.

We fall onto the bed together, tugging each other free of every stitch of clothing that remains. Griffin removes a condom from the pocket of his jeans and puts it on while I trace the grooves in his abs with my fingertips.

Once he's suited up, he moves on top of me, nuzzling my throat with hot kisses while the blunt head of him presses between my legs.

"You sure?" he asks on a shaky exhale. "We don't have to…"

Reaching between us, I find the right spot and moan when Griffin finally sinks inside.

He fills me completely and it's almost too much, but then he slowly withdraws as a deep gasp pushes past his parted lips.

"Holy shit, Layne. Baby," he rasps out the words like he's just as shocked as I am.

I never expected sex between us to feel like *this*. I thought it would be like scratching an itch, or like coming in out of the rain—I didn't think it would feel like getting thrown overboard into a tidal wave with no hope for survival. Because I'm sinking, falling … and there's not a damn thing I can do about it but make needy inarticulate sounds and grasp his muscles as I hold on.

"*Fuck*," he groans again, finding a rhythm that makes us both shudder and moan.

Seeing this side of Griffin is almost mind-blowing. He's so sexy and masculine and tempting … I don't know how I'll ever look at him the same way ever again. I'm pretty sure I'm always going to see him like this—long after he's gone—whenever I close my eyes—which is a dangerous thought. But I know I'll picture his wide shoulders holding his weight over me, his broad chest rising with each shuttered breath, his trim hips moving in deep, steady thrusts.

He lasts much longer than I expect—then again, I have no idea what I was expecting, because sex with Kristen's brother isn't something I ever envisioned happening.

It's only after he's wrung two mind-blowing orgasms from my body does he let go, emptying himself into the condom with a deep rumbling sound that he breathes into my throat. It's sexy and also tender. I love how affectionate he is during sex—kissing my lips and my neck and telling me how good I felt. And when it's over, he doesn't flee like I expect him to, he just hauls me up onto his chest and holds me until our breathing slows and I'm utterly calm and relaxed.

FIFTEEN

Griffin

Standing in front of the architectural firm that could make or break me, I feel lighter than expected. That's partly because I'm not carrying a thirty-pound massage table in with me and a duffel full of oils, lotions, and towels.

The only trace of my previous job is the faint scent of essential oils on my wrists. The earthy smell of eucalyptus always calms me, whether I'm nervous or just overexcited. This time, I'm more excited than nervous because I actually think I have a good shot at this position.

A month ago, I found the listing on a public forum for architects, and then spent the following nights tailoring my résumé and lining up references. Well, except the night I spent in bed with Layne

. . . I wasn't thinking much about job hunting with her calves slung over my shoulders.

As I relive the memory, I feel a slight tingle in my groin. *Okay, let's not get distracted.*

A classic Griffin smile has the receptionist in a puddle and me inside the executive's office in less than ten minutes.

"Jason seems to like you." Milos Ruben chuckles as he gestures for me to take a seat in the plush office chair across from his desk. He's a big deal in the architecture world, especially New York. When he set up an office here in LA, I definitely looked him up more than once. "I rarely get a smile like that."

"I'm sure his coffee was just extra sweet today," I say with a smirk. I don't mind the attention I get, whether it be male or female or otherwise. A compliment is welcome, no matter the source.

Milos leans back in his chair, splaying my portfolio across his desk. "I spent the morning looking at this, and I have to say I'm impressed," he says, pointing to a particular page that I was hoping he'd notice. "I like the teamwork aspect of this design you did for . . ."

"Cleanhouses. It's a company that specializes in converting abandoned, often condemned buildings into environmentally friendly shelters for the homeless. It was a pro-bono effort of my graduating class that I was lucky enough to take the lead on."

"That's impressive," he says, leaning one elbow on the desk. "You wouldn't believe how many of our clients ask about . . . what's it called?"

"Greener solutions."

"You bet. Twenty years ago, it was all 'how fast can you get me a design for my project.' Now, it's 'how fast can you get me a design, and how *green* can it be.'"

"It's a movement, certainly. That's where I spent most of my education."

"Perfect." Milos grins.

The interview goes on for about twenty minutes longer than it needs to, but I take that as a very good sign. Milos and I have a lot in common, from camping to our interest in self-care. When I tell him about my work as a massage therapist, he nearly shakes my hand.

"I've been saying it my whole life," he says, his voice deep with conviction. "The human body is the same as a house. Even the perfect design needs upkeep."

On that note, we end the conversation with promises to connect again at the end of the week. Jason waves good-bye as I walk out the double glass doors, feeling like a million bucks.

I nailed that interview. Dying to tell someone, I open my phone and scroll through my contacts.

Layne's number is at the top of my favorites, but I hesitate. I don't know exactly where things lie with us . . . we technically haven't spoken since the other night. I don't want to rock the boat, especially when the boat holds cargo as precious as my relationship with her.

Instead, I go to my number two, Kristen.

"What's up, baby brother?" Kristen's familiar voice fills my ear as I step onto the train platform that will take me back to my apartment.

"I just nailed a job interview, that's what."

"At the architecture place? Oh my God, yes!" Kristen cheers, and I can imagine her doing that weird little dance that she does when she's excited. "So, how soon before you can buy me things?"

"What sort of things?" I ask, humoring her.

"Kidding," she says with a laugh. "I'm so proud of you."

"Thanks. Yeah, it feels damn good to have aced this interview. I guess I'll have to wait and see what's next. So, what are you up to this week?"

"Well, Max did drop a hint the other day . . ."

"Okay . . . what sort of hint?"

"I think he's going to propose this week." Her voice is a whisper, but I hear the squeal of sheer joy perched in the back of her throat.

"Oh shit," I say, a dumb grin spreading across my face. "Are you sure?"

Max is a good dude, and clearly head over heels for Kristen. I didn't realize how much I approved of their relationship until this very moment. I'm excited *for* her.

"I mean, he asked for my ring size last month, and told me to clear my schedule this weekend for a surprise getaway? Like, it would be annoying that he's being so obvious about it, but he's so darn cute!"

As Kristen spills the details on the last few weeks of their relationship, I find my mind wandering to Layne.

Will Layne be this happy when she's proposed to? Will she have this giddy teenager reaction, when the man she loves asks her to spend the rest of her life with him? My heart flops back and forth between desire and dread . . . *I want her to be this happy. But not with another man.*

By the time I get off the train, Kristen and I say our good-byes, and I walk the rest of the way to my apartment with a newfound lightness in my step. I'm about to get a killer job, the job of my dreams, and my sister is about to marry the love of her life. *Life is good.*

So, when I see Wren sitting on the steps waiting for me, I can't help the sinking feeling, deep in my gut. *Why is she here?*

"Hey, Griff," she says with a smile, extending her long legs across the stairs. There's no way I can get into my apartment without talking to her.

I sigh. "Hey, Birdie."

She practically glows with happiness when I use the old nickname I gave her back when we were still in school. Maybe this won't turn into a fight after all?

"I missed you," she says sadly, her big eyes meeting mine. "Come here."

She beckons me to sit with her, and so I do. There's never really a good way to tell Wren no . . . not unless you plan to leave with your eardrums intact. Angry Wren is a *loud* Wren.

When I sit down, she spreads her legs across mine, knotting our limbs together.

"Did you miss me?" she asks, fishing.

"Of course," I say, and it's not entirely false.

I love this girl like a sister. We've been through everything together. We were even each other's firsts. Awkward and fumbling and completely unsatisfying firsts. And I would continue to love this girl if she would agree to some boundaries.

"What are you doing here?" I ask, training my voice to sound more curious than accusatory.

"I've been lonely," she says, using one bangled wrist to toss her long red hair over a pale shoulder. "It's like I don't have any friends other than you, sometimes."

Do you have other friends?

"Come on . . ." I scoff, unsure of what response she's looking for.

Suddenly, Wren attacks me with an embrace. She wraps her thin arms around me, nestling her head against my cheek.

Goddammit.

"Is this okay?" she asks, after the deed is already done.

I tentatively put my hand on her back, careful not to touch any exposed flesh beneath the crop top she's wearing. "Yeah," I say, not entirely agreeing with myself.

I've never been okay with how comfortable Wren makes herself around me. If she's not draped over me every moment that we're together, then something is terribly wrong.

Well, at least she isn't mad at me.

I squeeze her slightly, returning the embrace, and Wren sighs happily. She's such a loyal friend, even if some of her tendencies make me antsy.

"Aren't you going to invite me in?" she asks, poking me in the chest.

"I don't know . . . I'm pretty tired." On my way home, I was looking forward to making myself dinner and then calling it an early night. But Wren's presence puts a monkey wrench in that plan.

"We can just watch TV," she says with a pout.

This woman is in her late twenties now and still pouts like a child. I think back to Layne, pouting because we didn't have a condom. *Why was that so cute, and this so annoying?*

"If we watch a movie, you're just going to lay on me the whole time, and I won't actually rest," I say bluntly, giving her another squeeze as if to say, *We're still friends. I just need space.*

Wren detaches herself from me abruptly, putting several inches of space between us. "What's going on?" She's frowning, which is exactly what I wanted to avoid.

"I just need some space," I say, gesturing between us. "Like this? This is good."

She narrows her eyes at me. "Why do you need space?"

She's so pushy. Sometimes I feel like Wren brings the drama onto herself by being so difficult.

"I want to feel comfortable around you," I say with a sigh. "But when you're hanging all over me, it feels . . . I don't know, weird."

"Why is it weird? We've always been close."

"Okay, but what happens when one of us starts dating someone? Cora hated how entitled you were around me."

"I've known you forever. I'm allowed to be entitled. Cora was a bitch, anyway. She didn't deserve you."

"She was *not* a bitch. She was a really good person. I wasn't."

"Why, did you cheat on her?"

"No," I say, exasperated with Wren's prying.

"Then why did she dump you? Did *she* cheat on you?"

"No, Wren."

"You never tell me anything anymore."

If I wanted to tell you, I would have. "I'm allowed to have a life outside of our friendship, aren't I?"

"Of course you are. But I feel like I should still know—"

"Everything?" I say, interrupting her. *Okay, not wise.*

"No, if you hadn't interrupted me, I would have said *the important things*."

I purse my lips and clasp my hands in front of me, trying to calm myself down.

"Like right now," she says. "You're obviously keeping something from me."

"I'm sorry," I say, hearing myself apologizing

and unsure of what I mean by that.

"Are you seeing someone new?"

I don't speak for a moment. What's the harm in telling Wren? She wouldn't tell Kristen or any of our friends . . . I know that much.

I sigh. "Yeah, I'm seeing someone. I don't know where it's going, though."

"Is it Layne?"

I swallow. "Yeah," I say, meeting Wren's eyes. "It's Layne."

"Why didn't you just tell me?"

"Well . . ." I laugh wryly. "It's very new."

"I'm sure you're happy," Wren says, crossing her arms, but she certainly doesn't seem to be.

"I am happy. And nervous, and excited," I say. "I've been waiting for this—"

"For the past few years. I know."

Wren and I sit in silence for a while. I watch her pick at her nails and wonder what's running through her head right now. I've never been able to read her.

"Well, I'd better get going," she says suddenly,

vaulting off of the stairs. "I had a backup date in case you didn't come home or were busy."

"Good," I say with an encouraging smile, but she doesn't return it.

Giving me a serious look, she says, "Don't ignore me for another month, okay?"

"Okay."

"Promise?"

"Promise."

And with that, Wren leaves me on the front steps of my apartment building. I sit there for a while, my mind racing from the precious, fragile thing I have with Layne, to the volatile, stressful thing I have with Wren.

With a shake of my head, I rise to my feet and turn toward my door. I'm going to need more than pasta and a movie to decompress after that conversation.

It's never easy with her.

SIXTEEN

Layne

By this point, you'd think I'd be sick of engagement parties. Lord knows I've attended enough of them.

But today's engagement party? It's different. I won't have to sit through countless celebrations of a love I'm not sure is going to last, and do my best not to roll my eyes or burst anyone's bubble. No, this time I'll be celebrating a love I believe in, the love of my best friend who has truly found the love of her life. I couldn't be happier for her or more excited to spend today with the happy couple.

Plus, Griffin will be there, and honestly, things between us just keep getting hotter. I'd be lying if I said I wasn't ready to spice things up a little.

After giving my dark curls one last spritz of

hair spray, I check my makeup in the mirror, noting the way the classic navy shift dress fits over my curves. I'm not normally one to wander into boutiques and try on dresses at random, but I've been feeling more spontaneous than usual these days.

On the drive over to Kristen's parents' house, I'm surprised by the nervous fluttery feeling in my stomach. It's only been a few days since I've seen Griffin, but this will be the first time seeing him with all our friends since we started doing whatever it is we're doing, and I'm not sure how it's going to go.

We haven't told anyone about it, and I have no plans to. What would we even say? *"Hey guys, I know we've been friends for years and he's my best friend's younger brother, but we're fucking now. Yes, it's complicated, and no, we have no idea what we're doing."*

My palms sweat at the mere thought of that conversation, so I tuck it away in a far corner of my brain and turn up the music on the radio. That line of questioning is for another day. Right now? All I'm worried about is having fun and making sure Kristen has the best engagement party ever.

As promised, I arrive twenty minutes early to help set up the drink table and make sure Kristen doesn't have a panic attack before the other guests arrive. After parking in one of the few spots close to the house, I walk up to the front door, and to my surprise, it swings open before I can even knock.

Standing in front of me is a familiar turquoise-eyed tall drink of water in dark jeans and a gray sweater with a blue collared shirt underneath. He steps out and closes the door behind him, sweeping me up in his arms before I can say anything, and plants an urgent kiss on my mouth.

My first instinct is to panic, to resist—*what if someone sees us?!*—but Griffin's kiss drowns out all rational thought for a moment. I give in, looping my arms around his neck and softening into the kiss. But all at once, I regain my senses, pulling away and taking a few steps back, wildly looking around us to make sure no one saw what just happened.

What the hell did just happen?

"You look incredible," he says, a stupid smile on his face as he looks me over from head to toe.

"Stop that. You need to get it together. We're in public." My tone is terse, but on the inside, I'm melting.

I'd be lying if I said this new dress wasn't for him, and the fact that he appreciates it makes the extra half hour of primping and pruning worth it.

Plus, that sweater is doing his chest all kinds of favors—not that he needs any help. I know that from firsthand experience now.

"Everyone's out back. Don't worry." He shrugs, that stupid smile still glued to his face, sending electric pulses straight through me.

"Look, we have to be careful. Obviously, whatever's going on right now is still very new and fragile, and I don't think I'm ready for anyone to know about it yet." I have to avoid his eyes as I speak, not only because we haven't talked about this yet, but also because the longer we make eye contact, the less I care about anything other than letting him take me right here and now.

"You should have thought about that before showing up here looking like a fucking smoke show, babe."

Heat rises from my core, spreading over my chest and cheeks. It's all I can do to roll my eyes, doing my best to tamp down the arousal I so obviously and clearly feel in his presence. Taking a deep breath, I meet his eyes, my heartbeat going into immediate overdrive.

"Behave," I murmur, opening the door behind him and walking inside, my skin practically lighting on fire where our arms brush.

We walk through the entryway into the living room, where Griffin's parents' massive backyard is perfectly showcased by white French doors, left open to let the afternoon breeze move through the house. I knew Kristen's party would be impeccably decorated, but this is even more beautiful than what I envisioned.

White ceramic pitchers holding fresh flowers of all kinds are scattered throughout the house, and on the tall cocktail tables draped in white lace tablecloths in the backyard. Little touches of Kristen are everywhere—from the antiqued gold cutlery to the burlap runners. It makes my heart happy to see that she's truly able to give herself the engagement party of her dreams.

"You must be Layne!" a woman's voice calls to us from the other side of the yard.

I turn to find what looks like an older version of Kristen smiling by the drink table and waving me over. She's about Kristen's height and with her same auburn curls, only hers are cut short, framing her angular face, and her eyes are a warm, doe-eyed brown.

"And you must be Donna," I say, extending a hand when I reach the table. "It's so nice to finally meet you."

But when I turn to nod to Griffin, who I assumed was right behind me, he's nowhere to be found. Apparently, the whole *my new secret hookup meeting my mom* thing isn't something he's ready to deal with quite yet. Fine by me.

"The kids didn't warn you? I'm a hugger." Donna pulls me in for a warm, slightly awkward embrace.

I hug her back with half the strength she's holding me, forcing a normal-looking smile onto my face when she lets me go. "Your house is beautiful, and the decorations are absolutely stunning. It was so kind of you to open up your home like this."

"It's not like Krissy could have had a party this size in that apartment of hers. Could you imagine? We'd all be packed in there like sardines."

"Well, I know she appreciates it. Speaking of, where is the blushing bride-to-be?"

"In my bathroom, still getting ready. You know how she is. Actually, why don't you go check on her? Down the hallway and to the left."

"Sure, I'll check on her, but I'm sure she looks amazing. When I get back, I expect you to put me to work."

I leave Donna aligning champagne flutes to

wander through their massive Spanish-style home, the kind of place I used to gawk at while I was still dreaming of my own place years ago. All the warm tones and beautiful tile are making my home-crazy brain light on fire, but I tell myself it's time to focus. Time to make sure Kristen is okay, and not, like, about to pull her eyelashes out from nerves or something.

"Knock, knock," I say when I reach the bathroom.

I poke my head through the doorway to find Kristen leaning over the sink to see herself better in the mirror as she applies mascara. Even with her version of the silly mascara face we all make, she looks gorgeous in her cream-colored lace dress with delicate off-the-shoulder sleeves and mid-calf hemline.

"Oh, Layne, thank God. This is a disaster. Help me," she says, turning to reveal a gray streak running down one side of her face, presumably from the dreaded mascara tears she cried earlier.

"Okay, first things first. You look amazing. And second, this is totally manageable. You know I have firsthand experience at dealing with mascara tears."

She gives me a halfhearted smile as I join her

in front of the mirror, using a tissue to gently dab at the streak until the color is gone. Then I get to work, using her foundation to lightly cover over it, and within minutes, Kristen is back to her gorgeous self.

"You look really pretty," she says, her gaze flitting over my dress. "I haven't seen this before. Is it new?"

I shrug, dusting a soft layer of blush over the apples of her cheeks. "Picked it up last week. Just felt like refreshing my look a little."

"Well, I *love* it. What sparked the revamp? Anyone new I should know about?"

Damn, I wish I were a little less predictable. I didn't expect to have to tell a bald-face lie to Kristen anytime soon, but I guess this is how life just has to go today.

"It's not every day your best friend has an engagement party. I had to look good for my Krissy," I reply with a wink, a little surprised with how easily the lie slips out.

"Oh God. Please tell me my mother didn't hug you. I've been trying to teach her about boundaries with strangers."

"She definitely hugged me, but it was sweet.

Besides, even if this is the first time we met, I'd hardly consider the mother of my best friend a stranger."

"Okay, if you keep that up, I'm going to cry for real this time," Kristen says, her brows scrunching together and her eyes threatening to well up again.

"Fine, fine. I hate you, and this friendship means nothing to me," I tease, throwing my hands in the air.

We laugh, and Kristen checks her reflection in the mirror one last time before making her grand entrance.

"You really think I look okay?"

"You look incredible," I assure her, slipping my arm around her waist as we walk out of the bathroom. "Max won't know what hit him. And this party? It's going to be the best engagement party anyone's been to in years."

I wasn't wrong. By the time all the rest of the guests arrive, Kristen's parents' house is as packed and lively as LA's most popular brunch spot at eleven a.m. on a Sunday. But, if you ask me, the champagne here is even better.

After putting out a couple of small fires with the caterers, I convince Kristen and her mom to relax and have a good time—which means I can finally have a good time too. While chatting with a few friends I haven't seen in a while, I find myself scanning the backyard for any sign of Griffin. I find him by the drink table, chatting with some people I've never seen before.

As if by instinct, he glances over at me, his eyes meeting mine with the kind of knowing intensity that makes my stomach do somersaults. After holding his gaze for a few seconds, I have to look away, doing my best to look normal and casual in front of my friends. Even though, deep down, I'm totally freaking out like a high school girl on prom night, waiting for her crush to ask her to dance.

"So, Layne, I heard you bought your own place last year. That's amazing! And so brave of you to do it all on your own."

Liza Friedman and I have always been more frenemies than friends, and comments like that are exactly why. She's one of the women from the spin class where Kristen and I became friends, and while she wasn't always this outwardly catty, I've always had a feeling she wasn't quite as sweet as she first seemed. Luckily for Liza, Kristen's a more forgiving friend than I am at times. Plus, Liza's husband, Tom, is one of Max's best friends, so it doesn't look like we'll be getting rid of Liza anytime soon.

"Well, when the home of my dreams finally went on the market, I knew I had to jump on the opportunity. And it's not like I needed a partner to help offset the down payment," I reply, forcing a casual smile on my lips. I'm not about to pick a fight with this woman, but her passive-aggressive comments about my life choices make my blood boil.

"I can't imagine having all that space to myself. Although, I guess with the hours you work, you wouldn't really have the time to relax and enjoy it like we do," Liza says, wrapping her hand around Tom's arm and beaming a sugary-sweet smile up at him.

I'm about to ready to snap when a hand lightly touches my lower back, and Griffin's tall, strong body appears beside me.

"You know, that's a common stereotype about lawyers, especially women who have the balls to take on high-powered positions," he says, standing close enough to me that I can feel the heat radiating from his body. "But you'd be surprised how easily Layne manages her schedule. What's that saying? Work smarter, not harder? She's an absolute beast, and a damn good lawyer. I think we can all learn something from the way she leads her life." He flashes one of his charming smiles Liza's way.

Good God, I could rip his clothes off right here.

He clinks his glass to mine with a wink, and this time my stomach does a freaking round-off back handspring.

Liza doesn't respond. She simply smiles and changes the subject, but I can tell from the look in her eyes that she's been defeated. For now, at least.

"Thanks for that," I murmur, sidestepping away from Liza and her cronies. "Really. It means a lot."

"It's true," he says.

He's still standing close enough that my elbow tingles where it makes contact with his arm. I have a feeling that if I were to look him in the eye right now, I might actually burst into flames.

"I should probably go make sure we're not running low on canapés," I say halfheartedly, not wanting to leave, but wary of the two of us being seen together alone for too long. I make a move to turn to leave, but his fingers graze my arm, stopping me in my tracks.

"I want you so bad right now," he says, low enough that only I can hear.

"Griff . . ."

"As great as that dress looks on you, all I can

think about is taking it off."

I go weak in the knees, and for a second, I'm worried they might actually buckle. "Not now," I whisper, slowly regaining my composure.

"Then when?" His voice is low, seductive.

After a quick scan of the backyard to be sure no one's watching us, I turn back around to meet his eyes, my shoulders squared to his broad ones, my breasts nearly touching his chest. "Ten minutes. Meet me in the upstairs bathroom."

Before he can respond, I slide past him, finding a confused-looking caterer to direct back to the kitchen. I take one last look at Griffin before walking inside the house and am pleased to find a dumbstruck but definitely turned-on look plastered on his face, only to quickly wash away once some- one he knows approaches him to talk.

Again, as if he can feel me watching, Griffin catches my eye for a moment, his mouth twitching into a half smile as he lifts his chin with a subtle nod.

My stomach completes its gymnastics routine as I lead the caterer into the kitchen, pointing him in the right direction before grabbing a strawberry from one of the platters and making my way to the front of the house.

Checking the few rooms nearby to make sure no one will overhear, I walk into the upstairs bathroom. I glance at my reflection in the mirror, barely recognizing the woman staring back at me. My cheeks are rosy, and my eyes are bright.

The sound of footsteps in the hall makes my heart beat faster, and I swear all the blood in my body goes straight between my legs.

Griffin steps through the door, closes it quickly behind him, and removes the distance between us in one fluid motion. He takes my face in his hands, then slides them behind my hair and pulls me to him, our mouths meeting with more passion and urgency than they ever have before. The kiss is feverish, frantic even, as the sexual tension that's been building between us for the past two hours releases all at once.

He backs me up against the counter and lifts my butt easily onto it, parting my knees so he can situate himself between my legs. He presses against me, already hard and ready, ratcheting up my need for him even more. Making quick work of unbuttoning his pants, I slip a hand inside his waistband, and give his shaft a long, slow pull that makes him growl into my neck.

"Fuck, Layne," he whispers, trailing his lips over the delicate skin below my jawline as his hands run up my thighs and take a handful of both ass cheeks.

He squeezes as I delicately pull his swollen erection out of his pants, sliding my thumb over the tip. He hooks his fingers around the elastic of my panties, pulling them down and over my ankles so they fall to the floor. He produces a condom from his pocket and suits up.

All at once, he's inside me, and I gasp out a breath.

"Yes," I groan, wrapping my legs around his hips. For a moment, the world stops, and we're not two friends with a complicated past, and ten years between us, and all that other stupid stuff to worry about. I'm just Layne, and he's just Griffin. We're simply us—and it's so stupidly, wildly, unbelievably right.

Grabbing his shoulders for support as he thrusts into me, I do my best to hold on, but within minutes, Griffin is driving me toward an intense orgasm. I bite my lip to stifle a moan and hang on for dear life.

"Fuck, baby. Yes." He groans when he feels me start to come. A few more steady thrusts and Griffin's right behind me, following me over the edge with a hoarse groan.

My limbs wrapped around him, with him still inside me, I plant kisses along his neck as our breathing slowly evens out. He touches my hip, gently withdrawing, and when he pulls away, I already miss the feeling of him between my thighs. I want to stay here, just the two of us, and forget about the real world for a little while longer. But the music outside the door and the sound of distant laughter soon remind me that we have to go out and face it.

I step into my panties as he zips his fly, and he chuckles, watching my dress bunch up as I pull the lacy fabric over my hips.

"What? Can you think of a more ladylike way to redress after a mid-party quickie?"

He shrugs and shuts me up by planting another kiss on my lips, one that lingers long enough to send a tingle between my thighs. *Jesus, this man is making me insatiable.*

"I can honestly say I never thought I'd have sex in my parents' bathroom before," he says, looking around the room like he's seeing it for the first time.

"You might not want to think too hard about that one," I reply, grabbing a tissue to fix my smudged lipstick.

"Oh, trust me," he says, moving behind me. He

slides his hands over my hips and presses his body into my back, brushing his lips against the back of my ear. "I'll be thinking about that for a very long time."

I get chills for probably the thousandth time today, a smile spreading across my lips. "You're gross," I tease, mock rolling my eyes as I shake my head at his reflection in the mirror.

He places a kiss on the back of my neck, his hands roaming over my body one last time before letting go. "Guess we should go back out there," he says reluctantly.

"You go first. I'll be out in a couple of minutes so it doesn't look suspicious."

"Damn, who knew you were such a pro at this?" He cocks his head to the side, his eyes twinkling like they do when he teases me.

"I watch a lot of romcoms." I shrug. "Now go, before someone sees you leave."

He leans back in for one last kiss before quickly slipping out the door and shutting it behind him. I don't hear him speak to anyone as his footsteps fade away, so it seems like the coast is clear. I purposefully picked this bathroom because it's tucked far away from the rest of the party, and there's another guest bathroom closer to the crowd. This may have been my first time hooking up with someone in the middle of an engagement party, but come on, I'm not an idiot.

I give myself one last look, making certain my makeup looks normal. The flush from the orgasm has mostly faded, so more than anything, it looks like I just reapplied a touch of blush. And my curls were already a little tousled before, so a quick run-through with my fingers is enough to make them look normal.

With everything in order, I take a deep breath, doing my best to get back into the party mentality. If there's one thing I can't do, it's walk back out there all giddy and not expect my best friend in the entire world to notice.

Even if that's exactly how I feel.

SEVENTEEN

Griffin

When I told Layne that I wouldn't be able to stop thinking about what happened between us at my sister's engagement party, I wasn't kidding.

Last night, I dreamed about the firm press of her hungry lips against mine. This morning, I burned my hand on my coffee, too preoccupied with fantasies of her soft curves against my palms. Later in the day, I broke the tip of my favorite lining pen, remembering the distinct sensation of entering her. To say I'm distracted would be an understatement.

I pick up my phone to text her, because apparently I'm still the same thirsty fuckboy I was back in college. "Love struck," Kristen would say. And for once, I don't think I'd argue with her.

WYD?

I click SEND and lean back in my swivel chair in my home office, rocking aimlessly from side to side.

Without my permission, my brain hurtles me back into memories of that night with Layne. The way that dress . . . was it lace? Whatever, it was fucking gorgeous on her. Then that beautiful smirk on her face that I couldn't help but kiss, right before I left her in the bathroom. I've never taken part in such a well-executed quickie before.

I chuckle at the thought, my chest warming. Then my phone buzzes with her response.

> I think you just butt texted
>   me.

I snort. My thumbs fly across the screen of my phone with the ease of a millennial who grew up learning how to text before learning how to pay a phone bill.

> It's harder to butt text on a smartphone than you'd think. It's an abbreviation.

This time, the response is immediate.

I'm so old. Would it kill you
to type a sentence for the
sake of the elderly community?

I smirk. Layne is a lot funnier than she gives herself credit for.

Only if u stop calling yourself
old. What are you doing on this
fine day, Layne?

My phone buzzes almost instantly with her response.

I'm at work. Like I am every
                          Monday.

Okay, I should have guessed that. I deserve the sass she's dealing. I wonder if she's having a bad day.

Can I come visit you?

I toss my phone back and forth between my ink-stained hands, waiting for Layne to bicker internally with herself before she ultimately decides that she does want me to visit her and improve her Monday. My phone buzzes, and I unlock my phone hurriedly.

Only if you bring dinner. I'll
be working late tonight.

I can't help it . . . I grin. I have the makings for *pasta fra diavolo*, a meal I've been itching to make for someone special for a while now. Considering Layne is the only *someone special* I've had for years, this particular meal is long overdue.

You got it, beautiful.

The thin drafting paper on my desk ruffles softly as I breeze my way to the kitchen. I have less than two hours before the end of the workday, the ideal moment for me to show up with piping-hot dinner for her. God, I can't wait to see her face when I bring a full-on picnic to her office.

First, I need to double-check that I have all the ingredients. I rummage through my well-stocked cabinets for the necessities: olive oil, basil, oregano, parsley. It's all here. Maybe I'm still a frat boy in some ways—well, mostly my sense of humor—but I sure as hell don't have the kitchen of a college kid. I keep my fridge full of fresh ingredients and shop for groceries a couple of times a week.

I'm relieved to find some remaining cloves of garlic, fresh and fragrant, nestled away in my produce drawer. Deep in the back of my freezer, I find the ropes of Italian sausage I purchased from the local deli last week.

An hour's work in the kitchen results in a damn good-looking meal. And the smell . . . well, the heady scent of wine plus the sharp scents of garlic and onion have my mouth watering.

I pack away the pasta in glass containers, and add a bottle of pinot noir, looking around to see if I've forgotten anything. I decide to pick up a warm loaf of Italian bread from the corner bakery, and preemptively pack a stick of butter.

With about a half hour before the end of the workday, I make my way to the train, dinner arranged neatly in the satchel slung over my shoulder.

In twenty minutes, I'm back where my fascination with this woman all started, standing at the entrance of the chrome-and-glass building that houses Anderson and Associates. This time, I'm carrying a picnic, not a cumbersome massage table. The moment would only be a perfect full circle if I somehow managed to rub my hands all over Layne's naked back again.

Here's to hoping.

When I make my way to the front desk, Layne's assistant, Sabrina, is gathering her coat and purse.

She meets my eyes with a smile and gives me permission to enter with a sweep of her arm.

I tap my knuckles against the door softly before turning the knob. "Room service."

Layne is facing her computer, her eyes focused on the screen. She looks stressed, and something inside me clenches.

"Hey," she says, her voice hoarse from lack of use, making me wonder if she's been holed up in her office all day.

"Hey, gorgeous," I say, closing the door softly behind me. "You hanging in there?"

"Yeah," she grumbles, stretching her arms over head. "I've been buried in contracts and riders all day. I think you're the first person I've talked to."

"Well, I'm honored." I smirk, setting the hefty satchel on the coffee table where I once arranged my speaker and massage lotions.

Layne raises her eyebrows, sizing up the bag of mysteries with hungry, glazed eyes. "What did you bring me?"

"Guess," I say.

I walk around her desk to stand behind her, placing my hands on her slim shoulders. My thumbs dig into the tense muscles I find there, bunched up around her shoulder blades.

Layne's head drops forward with a moan. "I don't have the energy to guess," she murmurs, obviously loving every second of this impromptu massage.

When I find a particularly tender spot, I feel her melt beneath my fingertips.

"Griff . . ."

I play these games with her for a myriad of reasons, but mostly just to prolong the time she gives me.

Layne's stomach growls loudly.

Okay, it's time. I drop a kiss on the back of her neck, releasing her shoulders. Her disappointment is tangible, but I know how hungry she is.

One by one, I unpack the plates and silverware, and carefully unwrap the wineglasses that I secured with cloth napkins. With a hiss, the lid slides off the container of carb-loaded, flavorful pasta, and Layne sucks in a breath.

"That smells amazing," she says, rising from her desk to join me at the coffee table. She tucks her legs underneath her next to me on the floor. Her fingers rest on my bicep absentmindedly, and the touch sends shock waves through my arm and straight to my groin.

Fantasies of the other day flash through my mind in a heat wave that flushes my face. Instead of acting on them, however, I spoon heaps of *pasta fra diavolo* onto her plate, garnishing the dish with a warm slice of bread. Layne waits for me to make my own plate, but I can tell she can't wait to dig in. Incapable of relaxing, she busies herself with the corkscrew, pouring a full glass for me and half a glass for herself.

Making the mental choice not to fight her on that one, I raise my glass to hers. "To a hard day's work."

"To a hard day's work that isn't done yet," she says with a wry smile, clinking her glass against mine. She takes a sip, fork already in hand.

Watching Layne eat is definitely one of my favorite pastimes. I love how her lips wrap around a fork or a spoon, how her eyelids flutter if she really, *really* likes it. From the humming moan she makes when the pasta hits her tongue, I can tell it's a winner.

"Okay, this is good." She sighs, covering her mouth as she chews and speaks at the same time. *So fucking cute.*

"Glad you think so." I take a bite myself, and damn, it *is* good—the perfect balance of sweet, spicy, and savory.

We eat in silence for a few minutes, not at all minding that the only sound is the soft scrape and tap of forks against ceramic plates.

"Worth the break?" I ask, lifting the wine to my lips for another sip.

Layne nods vehemently. "Thank you for this. Seriously," she says, pushing her now empty plate away.

I meet her soft eyes with a smile. She looks grateful and much more relaxed than when I came in twenty minutes ago.

When Layne moves closer, I push myself away from the table. She crawls across the carpet until she's straddling my lap.

"You still look hungry," I murmur, tracing her cheek with my thumb.

"You could say that," she whispers back.

Tilting her chin, I capture her mouth in a warm kiss, wrapping my arms around her to hold her close. She kisses me with eager strokes of her tongue against mine in a wine-flavored rush. I drag my hands down the curve of her back, my palms landing on her ass and grinding her hips down against mine. I groan, my dick pushing against the zipper of my pants, eager for her.

"Do you have a condom?" she asks, taking me by surprise.

"That's not why I came here, you know."

She nods. "I know. But now that you're here . . . we might as well make good use of your visit before I have to get back to those piles of paper."

My dick lurches at that. *Fuck*. I can tell her brain is working hard—at what, I'm not sure. But I can't help but wonder if this little impromptu hook-up is because of the advice of her therapist about having more fun.

As happy as I am to supply said *fun*, part of me can't help but feel a little unsure about all this. Is that really all I am to her? But before I can process it further, there's a soft knock on her office door. Layne scrambles off of me, straightening her skirt as she strides over to the door.

It's Sabrina, still in her coat.

"Just wanted to check if you needed anything else before I left? Dinner, maybe?" She peeks around Layne to the table where our dishes are still spread. "Oh, I see that's been taken care of."

"Thanks, Sabrina. I'm good," Layne says.

I guess I'm the guy who takes care of dinner and supplies Layne with orgasms. It shouldn't bother me—it's what we agreed to, after all, keeping things casual and fun. So, why is there a sudden achy feeling in the center of my chest?

When did all this get so complicated?

EIGHTEEN

Griffin

I stare at the email on my phone for a solid two minutes before I fully comprehend the words. It's a message from Milos Ruben, and if I understand this correctly, he's offering me a job as an architectural designer on his team.

I roll out of bed, now pacing my room as I keep reading. Full-time salary, create my own hours, benefits package, and a plan to pay off my student loans? Am I still dreaming? He mentions some "out-of-town projects" that he specifically wants me to lead, which can mean a number of things. Is he just sending me down to Orange County, or is he putting me on a plane to Australia?

I quickly compose a response, explaining that I'd be honored to work for him but need some clarification. What does he mean by "out-of-town" in the offer? How much of the job will be away from home? Can I work remotely? I have so many questions for him, but these are the most critical.

I'm drying off from a hot shower, surrounded by foggy glass, when I hear the email notification vibrate on the granite countertop. I quickly tie my towel around my waist and grab my phone.

Griffin,

Glad you're interested. More details to come, but to summarize:

Our NYC office needs a new junior designer to help with upcoming projects. We will pay for your flight, a moving truck, and three months of housing so you can get on your feet in a new city. Take the next forty-eight hours to decide. Let me know.

Milos

I swallow. New York City? Working for Milos Ruben would be a literal dream come true, but I didn't expect this.

I stand at the mirror and take in my reflection. My stomach churns with the excitement of the offer. I've worked hard for years to arrive at this moment, and now there's a world of opportunity before me and nothing to lose.

Nothing?

My mind flashes to the woman who's been occupying my thoughts for a while now—really, since I was twenty-three. Four years of back and forth with Layne have only made me dizzy. But now it feels like the chemistry we've always had is finally catalyzing into something more solid . . . something more significant.

If only I had more time.

What if I leave, and I miss out on this chance to be with Layne for good? What if I don't leave, and nothing ever really happens between us? I could miss out on the job opportunity of a lifetime.

The humid air in the bathroom is suffocating me. Phone in hand, I head to my bedroom and sit on the edge of the mattress.

I need to talk to Kristen, but first, I type a quick response to Milos.

Milos,

I appreciate the clarification. Thank you again for the opportunity. I will confirm either way in two days.

Best, Griffin

I press SEND and immediately dial Kristen. Her phone rings eight excruciating times before I hear her lilting voice.

"Hi, it's Krissy! Leave a message, and I promise I'll get back to you when I get back to you. Whenever that is. Buh-bye."

Fuck. She must be with Max's family. They have a strict *no phones at family gatherings* policy—a policy I've never had any beef with until this very moment. I clear my throat, waiting for the inevitable beep.

"Krissy, it's Griff. I got a job opportunity, and before you stop listening and call me to sing my praises, it's . . . complicated. I'm stuck at a crossroads, and I don't know what to do. Call me back and help me walk through my options. Thanks, sis."

I hang up, contemplating my next move. I need to talk to an actual person, not a voice mail. I dial another familiar number in my contacts list.

"Griffin?" Wren's voice fills my ear, familiar and comforting.

"Hey, Birdie. Can we talk?"

"Of course, baby. I'll be right there."

"No, you don't have to come over. We can just talk o—"

"I'm on my way."

Wren hangs up on me, and I groan. That was a mistake.

I leave the bathroom to slide on a pair of dark-wash jeans and a black V-neck T-shirt. Wren doesn't live far from me, so she's probably already yelling at some unsuspecting Uber driver to drive faster. Was there ever a time when she wasn't the single most intense person I've ever known? *Probably not.*

Within twenty minutes, nineteen of which I spent staring helplessly at the wall, Wren is knocking sharply on my door. When I open it, she barrels inside, attacking me with a monstrous bear hug and nuzzling her face into my chest.

"Hi," she says, her voice muffled in the fabric of my shirt.

"Hi." I cough, the wind nearly knocked right out of me.

She takes a step back, looking me over as if to

assess the situation. *Me* being the situation.

"Sit down," she says, gesturing me to my own couch.

Okay.

She hurries away to the kitchen, and I hear the burners clicking and the tea kettle rattling from a distance. I chuckle. Wren would hate to be called a busybody, but she's honestly the worst kind. *The kind that thinks tea solves every problem. Lord.*

In two minutes, she's sitting next to me, handing me a steaming cup that smells earthy and dark, like ginger and cardamom. *Not my tea.* I wonder if she brought her own tea bags. It wouldn't be outside the realm of possibility.

"Tell me everything," Wren demands, leaning back into the couch with crossed arms.

I sigh. *Here we go.*

I tell her about the interview a few weeks ago, about how I thought I nailed it but didn't hear from them until this morning. I tell her about the job offer, and all the strings attached. I tell her about my reluctance to move to New York, so far away from this city I've come to love. All the while, Wren sits there, patiently waiting for me to finish.

"That's it," I mumble, my hands clasped loosely around the now lukewarm tea. I look up at Wren, expecting her to have a lot of opinions. Instead, she has an odd look on her face.

"What?" I ask.

Her look melts away into a beaming smile. "Congratulations on the job!" she cries, wrapping her arms around my neck. "I know it's what you've always wanted."

"Yeah . . ." I awkwardly pat her back with one hand. *Did she miss the part where I'm not sure if I'm going to take it?*

"Don't worry about the details. It's all going to fall into place. I'll help you pack up your stuff, and we can take the weekend to get everything in order. I'll be there every step of the way, I promise."

I rub my suddenly stiff neck with one hand. "I don't know if I even want to go, though."

"That's ridiculous. You're going. And if you're worried about being lonely, then I'll come with you. I've always wanted to live in New York City, anyway."

Fuck me. No. "Wren, you're not dropping everything to move to New York with me."

"Why not?" she asks, her face suddenly a few inches too close for comfort.

Goddammit. I thought we'd been through this.

"Because that's crazy. You have a life here."

"You're more important," she murmurs, her gaze soft.

I stand up in an effort to break the awkward tension she's determined to build between us.

"What?" she blurts out. "We used to talk about living together all the time."

"In high school, sure. When we didn't have any idea what our lives would be like."

"Sure, back then. But we're still friends, best friends, so we must have done something right. I want to start over with you in a new place."

"Wren . . ." I groan, scrunching my eyes shut in frustration. "When did this become about you? This was about me, not thirty seconds ago."

"And I want to come with you."

"I don't even know if I want to go!"

"Why?" she asks, throwing her hands up dramatically. "New York City is amazing. Why wouldn't you want to move to a new, exciting place and take advantage of this incredible job opportunity?"

I glare at her. "You know why."

"No, Griffin, I don't."

We stew in silence for a moment, me standing against the wall and her sitting uncomfortably on the couch.

"I think something might actually be happening between Layne and me," I mumble.

As soon as the words leave my lips, I realize how young and stupid I sound. This is embarrassing as hell. It doesn't feel great when Wren outright laughs at me, either.

"You're going to turn down a job because of *Layne*? That's ridiculous," Wren says, stretching her long legs across the couch. "I won't let you do something that stupid."

"I don't need your permission to live my life the way I want to," I snap, and Wren's eyes go wide. "I just mean that I was hoping for your insight."

"And you have it. I think you should take the job in New York. Fuck Layne."

"Don't say that."

"What? Fuck Layne?"

"Wren . . ."

"Fuck—"

"Okay, you can leave."

I stalk over to the door and open it wide for her. Wren narrows her eyes at me. I don't budge, even though my stomach is in knots.

Eventually, she stands, walking past me and out of my apartment. "I just don't want you to sacrifice everything for a woman who doesn't care about you."

I don't know what to say to that. The words sting in that way that the truth often can.

"I'll let you know what I decide," I say firmly. "Thanks for stopping by."

And just like that, I close the door.

Am I closing the door on this friendship, one that's gotten me through some of the hardest years of my life? I don't know. I don't know anything anymore. I feel like I'm floating through space, untethered and limbs flailing. Which way is up, and which way is down?

With a clammy hand, I pull my phone out of my back pocket. Time to face the inevitable. I dial Layne.

"Hello, you're on speaker."

I smile. It's an involuntary reaction whenever I hear her voice. "Hi, Layne."

At first, there's a pause on the other end. "What, no jokes? No, *oh, I'm sorry, wrong number. I thought this was the STD clinic*," she drawls, mocking my low voice.

I chuckle. I'll admit, that was a good one.

"Not today." *How do I tell her this?*

"Oh, is this a booty call?" She lets out a disappointed sigh. "Because I'm drowning in client portfolios at the moment, and it's not a good time, Griffin." I can hear the *click-clack* of her nails against her keyboard.

"It's not a booty call. I have something to tell you."

"Oh," she says in a chirpy surprised tone, then her voice lowers. "Oh no, do you actually have an STD?"

"No." I laugh, but it feels forced. "I'm clean. I, um . . . I've got a job opportunity."

I hear her fingers still against the keys. "A job? What job?"

"With Milos International, the group I interviewed with a few weeks ago."

"Oh my God, Griff! That's big!" The excitement in her voice would be contagious if only I didn't know the caveat.

"It's a great opportunity. Benefits, a student loan supplement program, new digs . . ."

"New digs?"

"Yeah." My voice gets tighter by the second. "That's why I'm calling. The job is in New York City."

She's quiet for a second. "Oh. Wow, that's a big move."

"I know. I'm not sure if I should do it."

"You absolutely should."

What? I feel like a trap door beneath me opens, and I'm falling.

"You think so?" I ask, but I don't recognize my own voice. My heart is pounding, audible in my ears.

"Yes, it's a good move for you. I wouldn't necessarily pick New York City for you, because the culture there is much less laid back, and their expectations are going to be . . ."

As she continues, rambling on about *the New York mentality* and *rent increases* and *x, y, and z,* my head is spinning.

Does Layne truly want me to go? Is this thing we have—this indescribable, kinetic *thing* we have—really that disposable to her? I focus back in.

"But on the upside," she says, "this will be a perfect way to pay back your student loans, and right out of grad school. You'll be surrounded by young people your age too. There are too many reasons to count."

"Right. Lots of reasons." My chest is tight, and I realize I'm clutching the phone so hard my knuckles are white.

What I want is a real shot with Layne, rather than be used like some boy toy. But if I move to New York, that'll never happen. And then there's Wren, who's all too happy to make the move with me. Wren, who I'm pretty sure would also like to take a ride on my cock.

Here's a twisted thought. Why does no one want my heart? It can mess with a man's head.

There's another pause on the other end of the line. It's so deadly quiet, I can't even hear her typing.

"Well, was that it? I have some work to get

back to, so . . ."

I laugh again, but this time it's hollow and detached. I can't manage anything else. "'Bye, Layne."

"'Bye, Griffin."

I hang up and whip the phone across the room. It smashes against the wall and then drops to the floor, its screen probably shattered, but I don't care. I bury my face in my hands, releasing a shaky breath into my palms. Dragging my fingers down my cheeks, I stare blankly ahead into my unknown future.

I guess I'm moving to New York.

NINETEEN

Layne

"Do you think you could elaborate on that a little?" Dr. Benson asks.

More like I'll elaborate on your face if you keep asking me that stupid question.

I've only been at my therapist appointment for fifteen minutes now, but I swear to God, after the first five minutes, it started to feel like an interrogation. I've never gotten upset or annoyed with Dr. Benson before, but I guess there's a first time for everything.

"Honestly, I don't know what else to say about it." I sigh, crossing one leg over the other on her green velvet couch and fixing my gaze on the bookshelf across from me. "What Griffin and I have is fun. It's casual and sexy and makes me feel like a teenager again. Those things don't exactly add up to *let's get married and raise lots of babies together.*"

"Then why can't you look me in the eye when you say that?" Dr. Benson asks from her gray armchair, peering at me over her horn-rimmed glasses, her brows raised, her voice gentle and nudging.

And that's exactly the problem. I don't want to be nudged.

I take a deep breath, trying to calm myself before looking her in the eye. "Because the idea that Griffin and I should be in a serious relationship is ridiculous."

Even as the words leave my mouth, I can hear the shadow of doubt in them. But honestly? I'm telling the truth.

Is there some small part of me that wishes he could be the kind of man I need him to be, to step up to the plate and be a supportive husband, and one day, a supportive father? You bet your ass there is. But I've known him for four years now, and I still haven't found any concrete evidence that he wants *that* kind of future with me.

I'm pretty sure that all along he was just looking to get in my pants. And news flash: he finally did that.

Don't get me wrong, I have no regrets on that front—the sex is mind-blowing, and even if it makes me a bad person, the fact that we have to keep it all a secret makes it even hotter. My point is, I'm happy with how things are, and there's no way in hell I'm about to start messing with it now.

"And you're sure that your . . . certainty on the matter has absolutely nothing to do with the fact that Griffin has a promising job offer in New York?"

Goddammit, I hate it when she sees right through me.

A pang of anxiety hits me at the mention of his *exciting new opportunity*, the same one I've been trying to avoid thinking about from the second he told me about it. I did my best to sound happy for him. Hell, I even encouraged him to go. But on the inside, a part of me split in half. He wants to leave, and just when things between us are picking up. If that's not a sign that he doesn't want anything serious with me, then I don't know what is.

I chew the inside of my lip for a moment, holding Dr. Benson's quizzical gaze before I finally break down. "Okay, fine. Maybe it has something to do with that."

"Mm-hmm. And how are you feeling about the

possibility that he might be relocating?"

"Oh, I don't know. A lot of different things. From a career perspective, I'm over the moon for him. Grad school is hard work, so it's great that he's seeing positive results come out of that."

I pause, hoping she'll let me off the hook with that answer. But who am I kidding? She's my therapist. And kind of a hard-ass. She never lets me off the hook.

"And what about other perspectives? Your personal, more romantic one, perhaps?"

I shift in my seat, re-crossing my legs, and stare at that damn motivational poster on the wall, the turtle my trusty focal point for those moments in therapy when I don't know what to say. Or in this case, when I don't want to tell her about whatever it is she might be leading me to tell her about.

She clears her throat so softly, she could easily deny that she even did it. But I know this move from her. She does it whenever I avoid answering. Another one of the subtle ways she likes to nudge our appointments along.

"Personally . . . I'm not so thrilled. I guess the idea of him leaving feels like an end to something that just started between us."

"But he might not take the job."

"It's a great opportunity. He'd be crazy to turn it down."

"That may be true, but why don't we consider for a moment the possibility that he *wouldn't* be crazy to turn it down. Can you think of any reasons why he might want to stay?"

Crossing my arms, I take a moment to breathe so I don't sigh for the third time in ten minutes. I'm trying to be mature and play along with this whole therapy thing, but the more she steers me in this direction, the less I want to play along.

"Look, I can see where you're going with this. I just don't think he's interested in turning this fling into a real relationship."

"Why not?"

"Isn't it obvious? If that's what he was looking for, he wouldn't be applying for jobs out of state. He'd be looking for opportunities nearby, or at the very least, opportunities that wouldn't make us long distance for an indefinite amount of time."

"Maybe he did. Maybe he hasn't heard back from those companies yet."

"Still, though. Why would he tell me about this one? Why would he even be seriously considering it?"

"Right now, Layne, I'm more interested in finding out why this whole subject is bothering you so much. Especially if you really don't think that the two of you don't have a serious future together." Her brows knit together as she looks at me with concern, and I can feel tears stinging at the corners of my eyes.

I know the whole point of therapy is to better understand yourself and all that shit, but sometimes, it freaking sucks. I don't want to tell her how I really feel about Griffin. More importantly, I don't want to admit that to myself.

"What do you want me to say? That I like him? Of course I like him. I wouldn't be sleeping with him if I didn't."

"Do you think it's possible that your feelings go beyond wanting to sleep with him?"

"I don't see why it matters what I feel. It's too late. He's going to New York. It's over. There's no future for us." I throw my hands in the air at this point, completely exasperated by this whole conversation.

I don't understand why she's making such a big deal out of this. What's done is done. He has a plane ticket and a job offer and plans for the future on the other side of the country that don't include me. It's over. Done with. End of freaking story.

"I understand why you might feel that way," she says, "but I'm not so sure it's as over as you may think it is."

"And why is that?"

"Because he's still here. And you still have time to give him a reason to stay."

"I guess I just don't know if there's a good enough reason. What if I force him to stay here and we break up in six months? Then he'll have thrown his future away for nothing."

She pauses, leaning her head to one side in a half shrug, tucking her silver hair behind her ear. "It's a gamble, sure. But wouldn't it be better to take the risk and find out, instead of spending the rest of your life wondering how differently it all might have turned out if you'd taken the chance and told him how you feel?"

I don't have an answer to that question.

With my stomach in knots, I leave Dr. Benson's office, still unsure how to feel. On the one hand, she made some good points about the fact that Griffin hasn't left yet, and there's still a chance that he feels the same way I do. But on the other hand,

I'm not exactly sure how I feel.

I've always cared about Griffin. He's my best friend's brother. He's been there for me through some seriously shitty times of my life. But then everything changed. Now there's a part of me that deeply cares about Griffin and wonders what a future could look like with him. But there's another, louder part of me that has such vivid memories of the absolute player man-child he used to be, the stupid little comments he used to make to me all the time, and the fact that we've been going behind his sister's back. Would the excitement, buzz and need for each other disappear if we didn't have to hide?

And yeah, he's grown up a lot in the past few years, but he's still twenty-seven. We're at totally different times of our lives with different goals and wants. At the end of the day, there are ten years between us, along with a million concerns and questions. And to be honest I don't know how willing I am to go looking for answers. Because it's possible I'm a big fat scaredy-cat, and all of this is going to blow up in my face, and even though I've dealt with my fair share of heartbreak, I'm not sure I could handle having my heart broken by Griffin.

TWENTY

Griffin

"It's a good move for you."

Layne's words are ringing—*loudly*—inside my pounding head. I press my palms to the hardwood floor, trying to brace myself against the spinning. *Fuck.* The bottle of Four Roses sits nearby, only a finger's worth of bourbon left at the bottom.

When did I end up on the floor? Goddamn, what time is it?

"It's a good move for you." Those cruel words are looping like a broken record in my head.

Yeah, maybe it is a good move for me, Layne. If I was a fucking robot with no emotions. But not all of us are heartless workaholics who only care about career advancement.

God, I've resorted to name calling. I chuckle, the alcohol in my system helping me ignore the sudden intense churning of my stomach. If I only cared about my job, if that was my only source of happiness . . .

I reach for the bottle, determined to put those last drops where they belong . . . inside my drunk self. Through double vision, I vaguely acknowledge my wristwatch, remembering that I still have no concept of what fucking time it is. I draw the watch closer to my face, tilting the bottle and spilling the remaining sweet amber poison on my jeans.

"Goddammit."

There's more where that came from in the kitchen. *If I can stand up.*

I squint at the silver clock face, both of our hands wobbling with the effort. It's 7:56 p.m.? *Fuck.*

Since Layne gave me her unwanted blessing, I really jumped the gun on this whole New York City move. I sent off my acceptance email to Milos within the hour, packed some of my more necessary shit in whatever boxes I had lying around, and argued with my shitty landlord about breaking my lease. I got everything more or less taken care of in record time. I even booked a last-minute flight—the 8:15 p.m. flight to La Guardia airport that I'm about to miss. *Isn't that just spectacular?*

I fumble with my phone, finally managing to find the webpage I need to cancel this ill-advised flight. I'll take care of rescheduling it in the morning. Or better yet, I'll still be drunk in the morning, and getting on an airplane will be the very last thing on my mind.

The drinking started when I made the all-too-familiar mistake of getting too fucking sentimental. I scrolled through old texts between Layne and me, ultimately landing on photo albums. There we were, moving her into her new place, basking in the sunlight on that fateful beach day, arm in arm with Kristen at her engagement party . . .

That last picture was the one that did me in. The glowing flush on Layne's cheeks was evidence of her happiness for her best friend. It was also evidence of the secret we'd just shared in the bathroom, moments before. The whole time we'd been sneaking around, I thought we were simply having fun while we got our bearings in our relationship. I guess I was wrong.

"I just don't want you to sacrifice everything for a woman that doesn't even care about you."

Now it's Wren's sharp voice that's digging hooks into my brain. I totally fucked things up with her too, didn't I?

I reach for my phone again, debating for a moment. *Is it worth it?* Whatever, she's gonna figure out that I'm wasted one way or another. Hiding anything from Wren is a pointless and juvenile game at this point in our friendship.

"What do you want?" Her voice is angry, crackling across the line with a rawness I'm far too drunk to even begin to navigate.

"Hey . . . you," I say. I lay my head against the wall, trying to steady myself. I'm gonna puke within the next fifteen minutes, and that's a bet I could win money on. Or I'm gonna pass out.

"What do you want?"

"Mmm. Would you come over? I'm on the floor." *Or maybe I'll just pass out and puke in the morning.*

"Why are you on the floor?"

"You have a key?" My eyelids feel so heavy. *When did I get so tired?*

"Yeah, I do. Griffin, are you okay?"

"Oh, not great. See ya soon, crescent moon . . ."

The hand holding my phone to my ear drops listlessly to the floor. I can faintly hear Wren's voice in the background, calling for me, but the darkness is already taking me.

When I come to, there's a trash can inches from my face.

"Come on."

A woman's voice softly coaxes me, distant in my ears. Before I can understand what's happening, I feel a warm, wet washcloth blotting my hands and face.

I open my eyes, focusing them the best I can. "Layne?"

A strawberry-blond braid brushes against my shoulder.

"No, you idiot." *Wren.*

"Sorry." I let out a chuckle. If I can't laugh at what a pathetic schmuck I've turned into, then I'll end up crying. And I'm not about to cry in front of Wren.

Jesus. The thought alone is terrifying.

"What's wrong with you?" she demands, holding my chin with an icy, claw-like hand, and I shiver.

"I'm cold," I say with a yawn.

In moments, Wren is back with a throw blanket from my bed, tucking it tight around my hunched shoulders and rubbing my biceps aggressively.

Her eyes meet mine. "Can you tell me what's going on?"

"I'm on a plane," I explain slowly, hearing the slur in my voice. "I'm on my way to the Big Apple. The greatest city in the world." That last bit sounded a bit more like *greatest shitty in the world*.

"Okay, so, no, you're not. You're on the floor of your trashed apartment. What's going on?" She hands me a cold glass of water.

I take a long, satisfying gulp. I could drink the whole glass, but Wren snatches it from me, willing me to respond.

"I should be on a plane," I mutter. "But I missed it. Whoops."

"You took the job?"

"Yeah." I sigh.

"Good. You should," she says with a definitive

nod.

I close my eyes. "Layne thought so too."

"Oh . . . you talked to Layne. That explains *this*."

I don't need to open my eyes to know Wren's gesturing at the mess that is me at the moment.

"She doesn't care at all, Wren. She doesn't care about me for a second."

"That's what I told you."

"Well, you were right." My voice sounds raw, low and gravelly, even for me.

"I'm sorry," Wren whispers, her hand finding my cheek.

It's a little warmer now, so I lean into it.

"Thanks," I say, my lips brushing against her wrist. I'm glad she's here. Glad I'm not alone right now. "Thanks for being here, Wren."

"I'm always going to be here."

I feel the press of lips against my temple, and then against my cheek. Then against my lips. *Fuck.* Wren, my best friend, is kissing me with both hands braced on my cheeks.

I kiss her back, because why not? Why the *fuck* not? Everything is burning to the ground around me anyway. I've lost Layne, I'm about to lose this job I literally just accepted, and I'm sure this fragile friendship is next.

I tangle my fingers in Wren's hair, tilting my face to deepen the kiss. She sighs into my mouth, pressing her body into mine until I'm flat on the floor with my best friend straddling my hips. I run my hands up and down her thin body, trying to find those familiar curves I love on a woman. There's nothing, which is fitting, because I feel absolutely nothing.

Wren must have been reading my mind, because her lips find my ear. "You can pretend I'm her, if you want. I can boss you around and treat you like shit and use you for sex. Whatever you want."

Her words are like a bucket of cold water dumped over my head. I shift my body so Wren loses her balance, sliding off me with a small gasp.

"Jesus, Wren," I growl, distancing myself from her.

The room spins the moment I stand, but I need to put some space between us. *Now.* I slump onto my bed with a wince. Headache's back.

"Why not?" she asks, obviously perplexed by the situation.

Me too, man. Me too.

"I don't want to. With you," I say with surprising clarity. If I were sober, this conversation would be a lot more difficult. Amazing what a few drinks will do to a man. "I never, ever want to do this with you. You're my friend, nothing else."

I look at Wren, praying she'll understand for once why I haven't entirely kicked her to the curb yet. I want her to know that I love her, but not like I love Layne.

I love Layne.

Fuck, my stupid heart aches so much.

I lie back in my bed, willing the darkness behind my eyelids to pull me into sweet oblivion. I hear the soft scrape of the trash can against the floor as Wren moves it within reach of the bed, followed by the clink of the water glass on my bedside table.

For a fleeting moment, I wonder where my phone is. I lift my hand, as if to say *thank you*, because I'm simply too tired for any more words. Sleep is rushing toward me like a tidal wave, and I'm not about to fight it.

Go on. Crash into me.

TWENTY-ONE

Layne

My phone buzzes from the bedside table, knocking me out of my true-crime documentary daze.

Dr. Benson has been encouraging me to find new ways to destress for weeks now, and Kristen swears these kinds of shows do the trick for her, so I decided to finally give one a shot. And while I totally get the appeal, so far, all this thing has been doing is making me more stressed out than ever.

Pausing the documentary, I lean over to see who could possibly be calling me. If it's someone from work, there's no way I'm answering. But to my surprise, it's Griffin's name that's flashing across my screen.

"Hello?"

But it isn't Griffin's voice that greets me. It's a woman's. And she sounds pissed.

"Hi, Layne? Listen, you and I need to have a little chat."

"I'm sorry, who is this?"

"He's in love with you. You know that, right?"

It's a voice I've heard before. Not one I'm super familiar with, but I know it, and it's driving me crazy that I can't place it.

Then suddenly out of nowhere, my stomach drops. I know exactly who this is.

"Wren, is that you?"

"Oh, so you're smart enough to recognize my voice, but you're not smart enough to put together how he really feels about you?"

"What are you—how who feels about me?"

"Griffin, you dumbass! He's in love with you. He always has been. I can't believe I'm the one that has to clue you in to this. Aren't you the one who's supposed to be a brilliant, high-powered lawyer?"

I'd be lying if I said that this news didn't shake me up, but I immediately have my doubts.

Sure, he's wanted to get in my pants from the

moment we first met, and yes, maybe things have taken on a slightly new tone since we started hooking up. But love? That seems a little extreme, especially given the circumstances.

"None of that matters. He's moving to New York."

"Nope, not even close. He's halfway to being passed out in the other room right now."

All right, what the fuck is going on?

"He's what? Is he okay?"

"No, he's not okay, and you're a fucking idiot if you don't understand why. He just gave up the biggest opportunity of his goddamn life because he doesn't want to leave you. If that's not cold, hard evidence of how he feels about you, then I don't know what the hell is."

Before she can say anything else I can't comprehend, I hang up, my mind reeling from all this new information.

Griffin isn't going to New York.

He's staying for me.

Because he loves me.

With these thoughts still swirling around in my head, I grab my purse and get in the car. I have to see him. I have to find him. And more importantly, I have to find out if what Wren was saying is true. My hands are shaking as I clutch the steering wheel, and my stomach is one gigantic knot.

By the time I arrive at Griffin's place, I've gotten my feelings at least slightly under control, steeling myself for the possibility that Wren was just playing some sick joke on me, that maybe he's not there at all, and I'll be walking up to an empty apartment more humiliated than ever. But even if that's a possibility, I know now that what I really need an answer. I can't spend the rest of my life wondering what might have happened if I'd followed up on a weird phone call.

After knocking, I wait a few moments, pressing my ear to the door to try to hear any sign of life. I can hear the faint sound of music, maybe a TV on in the background, and decide to try the handle.

To my surprise, the door's unlocked, and I swing it open.

The sight before me isn't at all what I was expecting—cardboard boxes piled in the living room, half-eaten Chinese takeout containers strewn across the counter, an empty bottle of whiskey poking out of the full trash can in the kitchen.

Upon further investigation, I find a note on the

kitchen counter:

He's hammered in the bedroom.

Stop being an idiot. – Wren

It might have been sweet if it wasn't so condescending. But that's Wren for you, I guess.

I grab a glass from the cabinet and fill it with water. The walk to Griffin's room reveals a similar scene—half-packed boxes, furniture moved around in odd places, the general disarray of someone beginning the process of moving out of an apartment. I take a deep breath before stepping into his bedroom's open doorway, the smell of alcohol letting me know that this is exactly where Wren left him.

"Knock, knock," I say, leaning against the door frame.

Griffin looks worse than I thought he would. More drunk than I've ever seen him, slumped against the headboard, a pillow tucked haphazardly behind his back. His eyes don't seem to focus when he looks at me, his work shirt rumpled and partially unbuttoned. The dazed look on his face would be funny if it weren't so out of the ordinary to see him like this.

"Layne? What are you doing here?" he slurs, swinging his legs over the side of the bed and starting to stand up, only to immediately fall back on the bed.

"I could ask you the same question," I reply, setting the water glass on the bedside table and helping to prop him back up.

He snorts and laughs, more to himself than to me, shaking his head and pushing his hand through his hair. "I'm gone, baby," he says, still stumbling through his words. "Gone, so far away. Forever."

"All right, well, let's get some water in you before you go, then."

I hand him the glass and watch him drink, still confused by what exactly is going on. Maybe the job offer fell through or something happened with his contract. If he wasn't such a proud, stubborn ass, I could have read through it for him and made sure they weren't trying to screw him over.

I find his phone in the bedsheets. The screen is cracked to shit . . . that's new. I enter the pass code I've seen him enter before, navigating through his email to try to find any clue as to what happened. Instead, I find a subject line from his airline that I wasn't expecting to see.

CANCELATION CONFIRMATION: FLIGHT 5505 LAX TO JFK

Wait. Cancelled? What the hell is going on?

"Griffin, what's this?" I ask, holding the phone in front of his face.

He squints at it and shakes his head. "Gone, baby. Totally gone."

"Except you're not gone, you're here. So, what are you talking about?"

He motions for me to sit next to him, and I do, leaving a healthy distance between us. He jerks his head to invite me closer, but I simply raise an eyebrow in response, and he shrugs. Instead, he leans in close to me, his face within a foot from mine, and I can smell the sharp scent of whiskey on his breath.

"The better question, Layne, is why are *you* here? You don't give a damn if I leave and move to the other side of the country. You don't give a damn about me. About us. So why are you here?"

His words send a pang straight to my gut, but it quickly fades when I see the look on his face. He's not angry. He's hurt. And pleading. He wants an answer as badly as I do.

"Of course I care." I bring my hand to his cheek, stroking the soft stubble along his jaw.

His sad eyes meet mine. "Then why'd you let me go?"

Shrugging, I sigh. "It seemed like a great opportunity for you. I didn't want to hold you back from chasing your dreams. I want the best for you Griff, I always have."

He chuckles, dipping his head forward and leaning his strong, heavy body into my side. "We made a mess of this one, didn't we?"

"Yeah," I say, leaning back into him. "I guess we did."

He lifts his head to look at me, his face now only inches away. His eyes are less glazed as they meet mine, his brows knit together with a softness I haven't seen from him before. I press my forehead to his, our mouths hovering for a moment before meeting. It's the tenderest kiss I've ever received.

When we part, he takes a deep breath, and I prepare for some grand pronouncement, some final statement about what's going on between us.

"I've got some bad news for you," he says.

My heart sinks. *Fuck, fuck, fuck.* Bracing myself, I nod for him to go on.

"As much as I want to make sweet, sweet love to you right here and now, there's a bad case of whiskey dick holding me back."

I burst out laughing, shaking my head. *Of course he's going to take this moment to crack a joke.* "I'm flattered, but that's not what I came here for."

"Oh, really? You weren't hoping for a little more of *this*?" he asks, arching a brow and making his best drunk attempt at a sexy face—which only makes me laugh harder.

"All right, Casanova, take it easy."

"Don't think I don't see you showin' up here all sexy. I know that's for me." Griffin takes a slow, lingering look over my body, and I follow his gaze over my comfiest leggings and favorite pullover sweatshirt.

I cock my head at him and raise my eyebrows. "If this is all it takes to turn you on, I'll have to start lowering the bar for myself from now on."

"*You* turn me on. Like clockwork. Like sexy, sexy clockwork."

A blush creeps over my chest and cheeks as our lips meet again, his heavy hands fumbling over my body. As much as I want for the night to progress further, it's clear that he's right about the whiskey dick. Plus, it's been a long time since we've spent a night together that would only be rated PG-13.

"I think it's time for bed," I say, resting a hand on his chest.

"But there are still things we need to talk about." The look on his face seems earnest, but he's still as out of it as ever.

I appreciate the sentiment, but something tells me Griffin might regret having *that* conversation in the state that he's in. "We can talk in the morning. I think you should sober up first before we have this kind of talk."

He sighs, mumbling something that I think is agreement.

Lying back on the bed, we crawl under the covers, our bodies curling into each other like two perfectly aligned puzzle pieces. He presses his lips to my forehead before going completely still, his breathing evening out almost instantly.

For a second, anxious thoughts about what tomorrow might bring start swirling around in my head. But Dr. Benson's voice rings through my mind, telling me to enjoy the moment, to embrace the time that Griffin and I have together, and to not over think things.

Him still being here must mean something, right?

I shake my head and push away the anxious thoughts, nuzzling closer into his broad chest, and do my best to focus on the feel of his arms around me, instead of my fear that in just a few hours, this could all be taken away from me.

The sun wakes me in the morning, sneaking through the blinds and cascading over my cheek with a warm glow. I roll over, happy to find Griffin's mess of brown hair lying on the pillow next to mine, his blue-green eyes fluttering open and finding mine.

"Morning, sunshine," he says, his voice gravelly from sleep. He pulls me into him, both of us still a little drowsy, and I rest my cheek on his chest, watching it rise and fall.

"How'd you sleep?" I whisper, a little worried about my morning breath.

"Like a drunk asshole." He chuckles, running a hand over his face. "Thanks for taking care of me last night. Sorry you had to see me like that."

I smile and shake my head. "You would have

done the same for me."

A smirk floats over his lips. "Oh, I *have* done the same for you."

"Shut up." I swat his arm with the back of my hand, but we both laugh because what he said was true. He has seen me countless times in all of my hot mess glory.

Things feel good between us—natural, even—but the weight of our upcoming conversation still hangs heavy between us. My gut is churning, making me think the anticipation is starting to eat through my stomach lining.

"Did I say anything weird during my bender?"

I snuggled closer, glancing up at him. "You might have mentioned whiskey dick."

"Oh fuck, I did, didn't I?" He shakes his head, covering his eyes with one hand. "I need to stop drinking."

I can't help but laugh. "Pretty embarrassing for you, not going to lie." I smirk, poking him in the ribs.

He squirms, then pokes me back, and soon we're in a full-on tickle fight, rolling across the bed in fits of laughter, trying to dodge each other's reach. Eventually, we land with him on his back, pinned beneath me as I straddle his hips. We pause, our chests heaving as we catch our breath, and he brings his hand to my face.

"This is a nice change," he says softly. "I'm glad you stayed over."

"I'm glad you stayed too."

He pauses, a serious look passing over his face. Then he looks away for a moment, as if gathering his thoughts, and when his eyes meet mine, they're resolute. Hopeful, even. *God, he's so handsome.*

"I stayed for you. You know that, right?" His voice is soft, and something inside me clenches. "I canceled my flight, and gave up New York, because of you."

"Griff . . ."

He shakes his head, quieting me. "I want a real shot with you, to see if what we have—this crazy, wonderful, mind-blowing thing—is as real as it feels to me because Layne, you're it for me. I don't want anyone but you. Today, tomorrow and forever if you'll have me."

Even as the words are leaving his mouth, I can hardly believe what I'm hearing. After everything that's happened between us, after Dr. Benson's encouragement that I should give Griffin a chance,

after Wren insisting that he's in love with me, after spending countless hours sneaking around and
hiding from our friends, in this moment, my mind
goes blank.

For the first time in a long time—maybe ever, if
I'm being honest—I have no idea what to say.

TWENTY-TWO

Griffin

My words hang in the air between us like a frozen speech bubble in one of those superhero comic books I read as a kid. Except there's nothing particularly epic about this moment. Just a grown man pinned beneath the woman he loves, in his bed, waiting for her to say something.

Anything.

Layne's mouth opens and closes without a word.

"You don't have to say anything." I whisper, reaching with one hand to smooth the hair back from her face as my heart begins to sink. I mean, I would love for her to say something, particularly that she doesn't think I'm delusional, and that she also wants to be with me. That would be nice.

"N-no," she sputters. "Wait."

I love the look on her face when she's thinking about what she wants to say. As a lawyer, she's extremely careful with her words, and that care most certainly bleeds over into her personal life. I'm only half-nervous that whatever words she ultimately chooses could potentially destroy me or could change my life forever.

"I'm trying to say this in a way that won't offend you."

Fuck.

"Just say it," I murmur, my throat tight with the anticipation of an impossible-to-swallow pill.

"Okay," she says, her lips turning down in that resolute way they often do.

God, I love her lips.

"Being with you these past few months has been . . . honestly, incredible. I've felt like I'm in my twenties again, but also older than I've ever been before. Does that make sense?" she asks, and I nod. "I guess what I mean to say is . . . being with you is fun, and exciting, and comforting, and shockingly *normal* despite all the years we were just friends. There's a kind of balance between us that I never thought possible. You wouldn't believe how many hours I spent in therapy unpacking all of this shit."

My eyes meet hers. "You talk about me in therapy?"

I nod. "Let me finish."

I close my mouth obediently.

"Since you came to my office and gave me that unreal massage, and then I found out you were Kristen's brother . . . I had trained my brain to see you as a kid. An irresponsible, infuriating little flirt who was too concerned with casual sex and would never be ready to settle into something serious. I repeatedly reminded myself of our ten year age difference every chance I got. But then you went and proved me wrong, you made me question everything I believed and the more time I spend with you, I see you for the man you actually are."

My heart clenches.

"You don't really fit into my preconceived idea of a lover. You're not like any of the other men I've spent countless years trying to unwrap and pin down and dissect . . . You're Griffin. Simple, wonderful, makes-me-laugh Griffin. What we have is easy, but it's not boring. It might just be perfect."

She meets my eyes for the first time since she

started this speech. I'm completely in awe of how jaw-droppingly beautiful she is.

"So, what you're saying is . . ." As amazing as her words are, and as much as I'm going to cherish them for the rest of my life, I'm going to explode if she doesn't get to the point.

"I love you," she says.

My whole body lights up. "You what?"

"You heard me," Layne says with a quiet glare. "I'm not saying it again."

I'd think she was truly fucking pissed at me by the look on her face . . . except for the slight blush to her cheeks.

"I'm not sure I did," I say, leaning up so our faces are close. I stroke her cheek with my fingertips. *Is this real?* "One more time?"

Layne looks at me through hooded eyes, licking her lips. "I love—"

I crush my lips to hers in a searing kiss. She braces her hands on my shoulders as I pull her down to the bed with me, a soft sigh escaping her as our bodies meet.

Every touch tingles with electricity, as if each individual atom in my body has come alive for the very first time. Our kisses turn from hungry and desperate to slow and sizzling, our limbs entwined in a dance we both know so well. Suddenly, she pulls away.

"So . . ." She gasps, catching her breath. "How do you feel?"

I give her a look that says *really?*

"I need to hear it," she murmurs, her gaze downcast in a moment of insecurity.

We can't have any of that.

I lay our bodies down, side by side, cradling her head in my hands. Her big green eyes shine with a purity that cuts right through me. This is going to feel *so* good to say out loud.

"How do I feel? That's easy. I love you. I've always loved you. From the moment I met you and touched your skin, I wanted to be with you. I've never met anyone like you, and I want to spend the rest of my life at your side, loving you, creating a life and family with you. You, Layne it's always been you."

With every word I say, more tears pool in her eyes. As they begin to spill, I wipe them away with my thumbs, and she smiles at me.

"Okay, where were we?" she whispers against

my lips.

The kiss we share next is softer and sweeter. It feels different than every other kiss we've shared before because this kiss is our first as an *us*. I'm hers and she's mine and I never want it to end.

"What are you grinning about?" Layne asks, her chin tucked into her big plaid scarf. She looks at me now with a familiarity that makes my heart grip.

How does it feel like we've been a couple for ten years, not ten minutes?

"I'm just imagining what Krissy is going to think," I say with a smile.

Layne and my sister had a standing brunch date that I'll be crashing. It's not the first time, and considering this new development in our story, it certainly won't be the last. I just had to hope to every god there was that when Kristen flipped out, it was in a good way.

Even if she's upset, there's absolutely nothing that can bring me down from this high right now. I've finally got my dream girl and my sister will have to learn to live with that fact. "How are we going to start?" Layne says, chewing on her lip, nervously. . Of course she's nervous. Kristen is her best friend and now she's on her way to admit that she's been secretly fucking her brother behind her back.

Yeah, that doesn't sound great.

I give her hand a reassuring squeeze. "I think we just start by coming clean. Open it up with the fact that we're together."

"And then what?" she says with a heaving sigh. "We tell her about all the sex we've been having behind her back for months?"

"Let's not focus on the details of our sex life," I say with a cringe. *Okay, even if I'm on top of the world at the moment, this is still going to be awkward.*

Within minutes, we're at the front door of the diner where Layne and Kristen usually meet. The bell on the door jangles as we enter, and we're immediately greeted by a hostess who leads us to the back patio, where we find a smiling Kristen.

"You're here!" Kristen exclaims, enveloping Layne in a hearty hug. Then she reaches over with one arm still crushing Layne to grab my shoulder.

"Baby brother, what are you doing here?" she asks, squeezing my arm through my jacket.

Kristen is clearly exhausted, overcompensating with energetic greetings. People say that wedding planning is all-consuming . . . but now I see it. The bags under her eyes, paired with the messy bun piled on top of her head—she's a wreck. Furthermore, she's completely missed the glaringly obvious indication that something is different between Layne and me and that we are standing in front of her holding hands.

"I missed my sister. It's good to see you haven't drowned in tulle and flower arrangements yet."

"Ugh," Kristen says with a wrinkled nose. "If you think that there will be tulle of *any* kind at my wedding, then you're uninvited."

We join her at the tiny table, pulling a chair from another table for me to sit on. After our orders are placed, Kristen turns toward me.

"So, let me guess. You two got drunk without me last night and crashed at . . ." Her finger trails from me to Layne. "Layne's place?"

"Griffin's place, actually. And yes . . . and no," Layne says, folding her hands on the table diplomatically.

Wow, we're really jumping in, aren't we?

"Whatever, I don't want to hear about it. I get

it, I'm not cool anymore," Kristen says, her hands raised in surrender. "I get engaged, and all my friends assume I can't hang anymore."

"That's not it," I say, taking Layne's imploring look as my cue to jump in. "I got pretty smashed last night, and Layne came over to take care of me. Did you ever get my voice mail?"

"Fuck, I'm sorry for not calling you back. You know what Max's family is like."

"It's totally okay. It's just a long story." With a nod from Layne, I dive in and tell my sister about the job opportunity in New York.

Kristen clutches her heart with one hand, her eyes wide. "Oh God, please tell me you're not moving across the country," she whispers.

The look of horror on her face makes me laugh. I love my sister. I really do.

"I'm not, I promise. I turned it down for personal reasons."

I don't know whether I'm the one who should say it, or if Layne should. I turn to her, trying to decide my next move. Just as my eyes land on her, Kristen's follow, and soon we're both staring at Layne, who turns a bright pink in no time. *Whoops.*

Our food arrives, giving Layne a moment to

gulp down some ice water and regain a little composure. If I weren't concerned about Layne's emotional state, this would be so fucking funny.

"Hold on," Kristen says through a mouthful of french toast, then stops herself. "No, wait. I don't want to guess. I want to hear it from you two." She sets down her fork and looks at us with her eyebrows raised. The table is deafeningly silent. "Anytime now. My food is getting cold."

I don't think I've ever seen Layne look so worried before. So I take a breath, reaching under the table to squeeze her knee before looking back at Kristen. "It's been a long time coming, but Layne and I are seeing each other. I'm sorry that we didn't tell you until now. It's been a complicated situation, and we weren't sure if it was going anywhere."

"I'm sorry," Layne blurts out, more agitated than I think I've ever seen her. "I should have told you a while ago, but like Griffin said, I was just trying to figure out if it all meant anything. I feel so horrible for keeping it from you. Please don't hat—,"

"And does it?" Kristen interrupts, expressionless.

Layne and I exchange a confused look.

"Does it what?" Layne asks, her voice so tight,

I want to hug her.

"Does it mean anything?" Kristen reaches across the table, taking one of our hands in each of hers, and I can feel the tension draining from Layne next to me.

"Yes," she says with a big, relieved sigh. "It means everything. Griffin means everything to me."

I can't help the stupid grin that takes over my face.

Suddenly, Kristen releases our hands, throwing her fists in the air with a triumphant cheer. "Waiter! Waiter!" she cries, waving her arms. "Can we get some champagne over here?"

Layne laughs. "I don't know if they do cham—"

"Oh, they'd better!" Kristen cries, reaching across the table to pinch one of my cheeks and Layne's.

"Ow," I say with a groan. I can't say I expected *this* reaction.

"You guys don't know it yet, but you just saved my honeymoon!"

"What are you talking about?" I ask, genuinely

confused.

"So, don't be mad, but Max and I had a bet. Since it was obvious that you two were hooking up, we put a bet on whether or not you would start actually dating at some point."

"Are you serious?" Layne's jaw drops. "I thought we were being discreet . . ."

Kristen barks out a laugh. "Hardly."

"What were the stakes?" I ask, so proud of my sister for this absurd intrusion of privacy.

"So, if you didn't start dating, we would spend our honeymoon on a beach somewhere stupid," she says with an eye roll. "But, if you *did* start dating, like I thought you would, we would spend our honeymoon hiking in the mountains!"

My sister is practically bouncing with excitement. While Layne and I stare in complete shock and wonder, Kristen shovels french toast into her mouth, humming happily.

"Now," she mutters through a mouthful of breakfast, "I get to wear those Lululemon hiking leggings I bought last year."

"I'm so happy for you," Layne deadpans, and I snort.

She's probably annoyed that she wasted so much emotional energy fretting about this conversation. Who knew it would be this easy?

"Thanks," Kristen says with a wink. "You guys are so fucking cute together. Don't ever break up."

I smile, taking Layne's hand. "Don't plan to."

TWENTY-THREE

Layne

"How's the ravioli? Everything you ever dreamed of?" Griffin's voice coaxes me out of my happy place, his turquoise eyes dancing in amusement at what I'm sure is an almost orgasmic look on my face.

"Heavenly. When you said you had something special planned for us, I had no idea you'd be feeding me the best Italian food I've ever had in my life. How did you find this place again?" I ask before putting another bite of the most delicious spinach-and-ricotta ravioli in my mouth.

"One of our clients is the owner. I guess her great-grandparents opened it years ago, shortly after arriving in America, and it's been in the family ever since. Seemed like the perfect place for a date night to me."

"Date night." I smile, tilting my head to the side and reaching for his hand over the white tablecloth. "I've got to say, it's nice to not have to be sneaking around all the time anymore."

"Turns out there are all kinds of things you can do once you're an official couple," he says, lacing his fingers between mine as he flashes me a devilish grin. "But you have to admit, the sneaking around was hot as hell."

I chuckle at him and shake my head. "Are you worried we'll lose the spark now that we've gone public?" I pull my hand away and arch a challenging brow, crossing my arms and resting my elbows on the table, aware of how this movement will show off my already ample cleavage even more.

"Just say the word, and I'll meet you in the bathroom for a quickie."

We both laugh, and he reaches across the table to rub his calloused thumb along my cheek, sending a whole flurry of butterflies swarming low in my belly.

You'd think that our history together would make our relationship feel as normal as anything else—and in some ways it does. We got to skip the awkward *getting to know you* phase, as well as the part where you learn each other's quirks, both good and bad. But surprisingly enough, since we've made our relationship official, our connection feels as fresh and exciting as ever. Even more so because we now know exactly where each other stands. And since Griffin started working for a new architecture firm downtown and has gotten busier, our time together feels even more precious.

As Griffin sips his wine, I take a moment to admire this man I love—his straight nose, his cheekbones, his perfectly chiseled jaw accentuated by the slightest hint of a five o'clock shadow. It sometimes still blows my mind that I'm the woman he wants to be with. It's not an issue of self-esteem—I know how amazing I am, and he makes damn sure to tell me.

"So, have you decided what you want to do about the appointment? I think we should just hear what the doctor has to say," he says, resting his elbows on the table.

Leave it to Griffin to practically read my mind and ask a question that totally blows any doubts I have about our relationship out of the water.

I sigh, pushing my fingers through my hair. "I don't know, babe, a fertility clinic? I get what Dr. Trager was saying; I'm no spring chicken. And I know that I want kids, but jumping straight into fertility counseling feels so . . . defeatist. Maybe I should just reschedule."

I've had this appointment set up since before we started dating. It was something I felt the need to explore, but now that we're together, I feel less sure. I don't want to drag Griffin through this.

"I hear you, but I think it might be good to just go. At the very least, we can get some information and prepare for the future. Nothing definite has to happen right now."

He's right. I know he's right. But that doesn't change the way I feel.

"I'm just so worried that the second I walk in there, it's going to be bad news after more bad news. I already know that my age is an issue. What if there's something else wrong with my body that I don't even know about?"

"Babe, your body is perfect. Dr. Trager said he's hopeful it will all go smoothly," Griffin says, taking my hand again and squeezing it. "No matter what life throws at us, we're together. I'll always be right there by your side and we'll weather it all together." Tears well up in the corners of my eyes as he speaks. I know it sounds cheesy, but hearing him say those things out loud—even though he's expressed them before—means the world to me.

"I love you," I say, leaning across the table for

a kiss. "Remind me again why we didn't just get together and get this ball rolling earlier?"

He arches an eyebrow and raises his hand in the air. "I was on board from the second I laid eyes . . . and hands on you. Someone just took a while to come around."

"Yeah, well, someone *else* had quite a bit of growing up to do, if I remember correctly." I smile.

We hold each other's gaze for a moment, and soon we're both smiling. There's no point in playing the *should have, would have* game. We're together now, and that's all that matters.

Besides, I'm totally right about the growing-up part.

The next morning, the two of us are sitting in a waiting room, minimally decorated with pale yellow walls, steel-gray furniture, and a corkboard full of baby pictures covering one of the walls.

Nerves fill my stomach as a thousand worried thoughts race through my mind. I can feel myself starting to spiral out of control with anxiety, so I quickly grab one of the pamphlets on the table in front of me at random and flip it open, only to be faced with way too much information about fertility, which only stresses me out more.

Just as I'm on the verge of panicking, Griffin places a calming hand on my knee and leans over to kiss me on the cheek. "Hey, you okay?"

I take a deep breath and nod slowly. "I'm fine. Everything's fine. The reality of everything is just hitting me all at once, I think."

"No matter what happens, I'm here. You know that, right?"

I keep nodding, grab his hand, and squeeze tight. Honestly, it's strange how much I'm freaking out right now. I own my own law firm, for goodness' sake. You'd think I'd know how to manage stress by now.

It's going to be fine, right? It has to be.

After a few moments of deep breathing, and with Griffin's calming voice and presence by my side, I already start to feel a little better. As my thoughts begin to slow down, I take in the other patients waiting with us.

There are a couple of women who are visibly pregnant—one who looks about ready to pop, and another who's just starting to show. The first woman has a partner with her, a woman, holding her hand

and flipping through an important-looking folder. The other woman, though, the one who's just starting to show, is all on her own, and my heart breaks a little for her. Sure, I don't know her story. Maybe she has a partner who just couldn't make it to this appointment with her. But the thought that she might be going through her own fertility journey with no one by her side, no one to hold her hand, makes me incredibly grateful for the partner I've found in Griffin, and how encouraging and helpful he's been to me already.

"Thank you." I turn and place a kiss on his cheek. "I don't think I'd be able to do this without you."

"No, thank *you*. I know you were unsure about coming here, and I'm proud of you for following through with this. And for letting me be a part of it."

Our lips meet again, and when we part, I lay my head on his shoulder.

"Besides," he says, running his fingers over my upper arm. "I've got a few questions of my own for this doctor."

"Oh, you do, do you?"

"Mm-hmm. Let's just say she and I need to have a little chat about superpowers."

We laugh, and I swat his chest with the back of my hand.

"Behave in there," I warn.

"You're the boss," he replies, raising his hands in surrender.

"Layne Anderson?" The nurse reads my name from her clipboard, looking up and searching the room.

I wave, and she motions for us to join her. Griffin and I turn to look at each other, his eyebrows raised, a smile forming on his lips.

"You ready?"

I place a kiss on his lips and give his hand a firm squeeze. "Let's do this."

TWENTY-FOUR

Griffin

Sunlight streams in through the stained-glass windows, pouring a rainbow of colors on us. Standing across from Layne in this church is a truly spiritual experience.

Her long dress touches the floor, and her hair hangs in loose waves over her bare shoulders. Her eyes are bright and clear. She's unbelievably gorgeous. Gazing at her, sharing that secret smile . . . I may be the happiest man alive.

Well, no. Max is probably the happiest man alive considering he's about to marry my compassionate, badass, completely self-sufficient sister. Speaking of gorgeous, my sister really pulled herself together. The hours she spent locked away in the dressing room with Layne certainly paid off. She looks like a mermaid princess or something. I don't know how we can possibly be related.

Max's best man, Tom, passes him a tissue, and Layne does the same for Kristen. The bride and groom have tears streaming down their faces, almost to a comical degree. I catch Layne's eye with a look that says *what's going on here?* She smiles and shrugs in response. True love, I guess.

When vows and rings are exchanged, the minister finally ends with the classic, "You may kiss the bride." The kiss is passionate, not as chaste as our parents probably would have liked, which honestly makes it so much better.

I cheer loudly, and soon everyone in the church is clapping and smiling. The music starts, and one by one, all the couples in the bridal party make their way down the aisle and back to the lobby. I manage to steal Layne from Tom, passing off his wife, Liza, to him in a decently executed twirl.

Catching Layne by the wrist, I pull her close to me with a kiss. She outright giggles, a sound I've come to know and love. Architecture is great and all, but it's my life's passion to make Layne Anderson laugh at least ten times a day.

With all the attention on Max and Kristen, it's easy for me to pull Layne away to find one of the many dark crevices in the historic hotel where the reception is being held following the ceremony.

Layne follows close behind; we've got this quickie operation down to a science at this point. Once voices are far enough away, I push Layne against the wall and press my body into hers. She smirks at me, her eyes still a dazzling green in the dim light of this hall.

I open the door to a nearby conference room, pleased it find it unlocked, and we slip inside.

"Here?" she asks, one eyebrow raised.

"You followed me here."

"I guess I did." Layne grinds her hips against the front of my pants, making my already stiff shaft swell even more.

I lean in and plant searing kisses on her neck, pulling the straps of her dress aside to reveal her perfect breasts. I fucking love it when she doesn't wear a bra. As her hands massage my neck and scalp, mine ghost soft touches across her ribs and pebbled nipples. Her right hand rubs eagerly against my erection, which aches to be released from my pants.

I take a step back from her, undoing my belt, button, and zipper as quickly as I can. I can't keep my eyes off of her, pressed up against the wall, half-naked and dazed. She's hotter than ever like this.

Before I can register what's happening, Layne drops to her knees in front of me, taking me into her hot, wet mouth. I groan, grabbing her hair in my fist. She suddenly stops, looking up at me with a frown.

"Easy on the hair. We've still got to take more pictures."

I let out a breathless laugh. "Sorry."

She resumes sucking and licking my dick, working me into a state that I'm not sure I'll recover from if I let her continue for much longer. *Goddam.*

"Get up here, sexy." I help Layne to her feet and drop to my knees.

My turn.

I remove her heels one by one, kissing trails up her legs and lifting the skirt of her dress until my tongue finds her slick, sweet center. I draw lazy circles with the tip of my tongue against her clit, increasing intensity with every approving moan. Finally, once her breathing starts to hitch and her fingernails dig into my shoulders through my shirt, I stand. With my hands on her hips, I guide my cock to her center, driving into her at an excruciatingly slow and steady pace. We both groan, the sensation of flesh on flesh almost too much to bear.

I hold her ass up, giving myself the leverage to give her exactly what she needs—my cock deep inside her. She cries out loudly with every thrust, her voice echoing in the empty conference room.

"F—fuck, Griff, fuck," she moans, her voice breathy and desperate.

"Kiss me." I groan into her cheek, and her lips find mine in a hungry press.

Moments later, we both shatter into a million shimmering pieces at the very same time. Shuddering, I hold her body close, enjoying the final waves of pleasure as they rock through me.

Once we've both found our way back to reality, I set her down on the floor again. One by one, I replace each beautiful foot into a high heel. Rising to my feet, I zip up my own pants. Wordless, we help each other with hair and wrinkled clothes, smoothing out all evidence that anything smutty just occurred in a boardroom, of all places.

"I've got to fix my makeup before we head back," she says, peering into the darkened mirrored surface of a window.

"Sure," I say. "I think there was one just around the corner."

"Perfect." She smiles, giving me a quick peck on the lips before disappearing into a restroom down the hall.

I take a deep breath, reaching into my pocket to make sure . . . *Yes, it's still there.*

I hear the rush of water come from the restroom and take position. The restroom door creaks open, and her heels click down the hall as she returns.

"Griff, did you bring a pen? I think it would be nice if we wrote them—" Layne walks back into the boardroom to see me on one knee, presenting a glimmering ring. "Oh my God."

"Layne, baby? I have something to ask you—"

"Griffin! Are you kidding me?" She's shocked to tears, laughing with uneven breath. "Right after I leave the bathroom?"

"You can make up something more romantic to tell our friends," I say with a smirk. "I just couldn't wait any longer. I want to spend the rest of my life with you. Marry me, honey?"

Layne drops to my level, planting a kiss on me that's hard and tender at the same time. "Yes," she murmurs into my lips. "I'll marry you."

EPILOGUE

Layne

Two years later

Walking through the garage door, I'm immediately greeted by a fluffy black-and-white fur ball, jumping up on his hind legs to paw and lick at my knees, his tail wagging like crazy.

"Well, hi there, Scooty-Scoots. How are you? How was your day?" I coo at him, closing the door behind me and squatting down to pet him.

Scooter rolls over onto his back so I can scratch his belly, and I happily do so. I love coming home to this little ball of love after a long day at work—even if it was only a half day. But there's someone else I'm more excited to see right about now. Well, three other people, actually.

"Babe, is that you?"

I follow Griffin's voice into the kitchen, where he's sitting at the table feeding our twin daughters who are both strapped into a special twins high chair and dressed adorably in matching pink-and-white-striped onesies. My heart gives a little lurch.

"Hi, sorry I'm a little late. There was an issue with one of our contracts, but I handled it. Are those the onesies my mom got them? They're so cute."

I plant a quick kiss on his mouth before kissing each of the twins' chubby little cheeks as well. Both girls gurgle happily at me, evidence of the sweet potato they've been eating clinging to their chins and cheeks. One smear of it is across Georgia's forehead.

"Don't sweat it, babe. We're just glad you're here now." Griffin drops a sprinkling of dry cereal in front of each of the girls before smiling up at me, contentment in his eyes.

I lean down and kiss him again, longer and deeper this time, running my fingers through the back of his hair.

"What was that for?" he asks when we part, a sexy smile spreading across his face.

"I missed you," I say, hanging my tote bag on

the back of his chair and sitting down next to him.

"We missed you too. Even if it's only been six hours."

"Yeah, well, at their age, six hours feels like six years. I swear they've grown since I left this morning. Does Georgia's hair look a little red to you? She gets that from your side, you know."

"Maybe a little. But Charlotte definitely has your pretty green eyes. She's a lucky girl." Griffin slips his arm around my waist, squeezing me tightly as we watch our twins eat, fully consumed by love and gratitude for the family we've made together.

As if on cue, Charlotte reaches for Georgia's Cheerios and steals one, and both of them start crying. Griffin and I each grab a baby, clean them up and calm them down, rocking and cooing and telling them it's all going to be okay. Once they're settled, the four of us snuggle on our oversized couch, where the twins begin to drift off to sleep on our chests.

Scooter, the dog we rescued as a puppy shortly after getting married, curls up next to Griffin on the couch, completing our currently family of five, Scooter included. We got lucky with his temperament—the shelter wasn't exactly sure what he's a mix of. Not that we cared, then or now. He was perfect practice for us before the twins were born, and he's matured enough since then to be kind and gentle with them now.

"Never a dull moment with these two," Griffin says, shaking his head as he smiles down at Charlotte resting against his chest.

I smooth Georgia's hair and whisper, "Were they okay while I was gone?"

"They weren't happy about getting those onesies on, but besides that, they were a dream. I kept them entertained with my new comedy routine."

I chuckle and roll my eyes. Griffin has fully embraced being a dad, and for him, that includes constantly coming up with as many awful dad jokes as he possibly can—and making us listen to them, and making the girls giggle and me belly laugh.

"They only laugh so you don't feel bad about yourself. You know that, right?" I tease, loving that we can still tease and taunt each other like we did before we become a couple.

"Oh, please. They have their daddy's sense of humor. They know talent when they see it and don't you pretend that you don't like my jokes."

"Sure, babe, whatever you say. Speaking of talent, has Wren gotten back to you about this weekend?"

"Not yet. She said she was waiting on a new supplier."

"A supplier? She makes balloon animals and paints faces. "How intense can this business be?"

"I guess she uses only organic, all-natural products, and those can be pretty tough to come by in her industry."

"Well, tell her it's the twins' first birthday party, not high tea with the queen of England. We'd just like to have her there."

He smiles warmly. "On it. Did you see the picture Kristen posted yesterday? She looks like she's ready to pop."

"I know, poor thing. A week past her due date already. You couldn't pay me enough to be *that* pregnant again."

Griffin raises an eyebrow at me. "Are you sure about that? Because Charlotte, Georgia, and I were talking about it today, and they said they wanted a little brother."

"Oh, did they?" My mouth twitches into a smile and butterflies circle my belly like they always do when Griff mentions anything about babies. "Well, we'll just have to see about that, won't we?"

Before we can continue the conversation, my phone starts ringing from inside my tote in the kitchen. I get up, carefully place Georgia in her bassinet, and jog as quickly and quietly as I can to answer it. I pick up my phone and glance at Griffin after viewing the name on the screen.

Who is it? he mouths, and I simply force a smile in response.

"Hi, Mom. What's up?"

"Hi, sweetie. How are the girls?"

"The girls are great. Sleeping, actually."

"Griffin was kind enough to send me a picture of them wearing the adorable little onesies I got them. I could just eat them up, they're so stinking cute. Does Georgia's hair look like it's getting a little red to you?"

"I was just saying that same thing to Griff. Also, hi, we're fine too, by the way. Slightly sleep deprived, but we've got a good system going."

"Well, I'm glad to hear that, sweetheart. So, anyway, I wanted to call and go over some details about this weekend."

I walk back over to the couch and curl up next

to Griffin and the babies. As my mother rambles on about cupcakes and decorations, I make eye contact with Griffin, who furrows his brow to ask what she's talking about. I simply shrug and roll my eyes in response. *The party*, I mouth. He shakes his head and raises his eyebrows, adjusting Charlotte's positioning on his chest.

My mom has quickly taken to being a grandma, and while I'm incredibly appreciative of all her love and support, she's proven to be a bit . . . overeager. I guess I shouldn't be surprised—being a grandma has been her dream for decades, and now that she finally is one, she's taking the role very seriously. And lately, that includes commandeering the twins' first birthday party.

"And I was thinking maybe instead of peonies, we go with begonias—big, white, beautiful begonias. What do you think?"

She's barely taken a single breath between sentences, and I've learned to just go along with whatever she says at this point. It's not like I have some grand vision for what this birthday party needs to look like. I'm just happy that my babies are healthy and growing, and that our family is stronger than ever. If my mom wants to take over hammering out some of the details, that's perfectly fine by me.

"Begonias sound beautiful, Mom. That's a

great idea."

Griffin scrunches his eyebrows together and mouths, *Begonias?*

I shrug and shake my head, trying not to laugh at his reaction. Georgia's perfect little mouth stretches into a small "o" as she yawns, her eyelids fluttering open.

"Mom, I'm sorry, I've got to go. Georgia's waking up from her nap."

"Oh, all right, sweetheart. Give the babies kisses for me. I'll send you an email with the rest of the details."

"Okay. 'Bye, Mom."

Picking Georgia up and setting her in my lap, I snuggle up next to Griffin and Charlotte, just as Charlotte starts opening her eyes too. Our girls have such a strong twin connection sometimes, it's almost freaky. But we're getting used to it—and it's just one more thing to love about the life we've built together.

"I'm starving," I say, my stomach grumbling. "Do we have any leftovers from last night?"

"No need. There's a Sonoma chicken sandwich waiting for you in the fridge. Extra poppy seed dressing, salt and vinegar chips, and all," Griffin says casually as he makes a silly face to make the girls laugh.

It's a small gesture, but in that moment, the fact that he bought me lunch—my favorite sandwich, no less, from all those years ago—makes my heart warm with happiness. Tears well up in my eyes.

When I don't respond, Griffin turns to look at me, a confused and worried look crossing his face when he sees I'm on the brink of tears.

"Whoa, babe, are you okay?"

"I just love you," I say, leaning in and pressing my face into his neck, the tears falling down my cheeks as I close my eyes.

"Guess I should buy you lunch more often," he says when we part.

All I can do is laugh and shake my head at this sweet, thoughtful husband of mine, who does these small, kind things for me without even realizing how meaningful they are.

"By the way," he adds as I stand with Georgia on my hip. "Don't think I've forgotten about the whole *little brother for the twins* conversation."

"I haven't either. Let's get through this party first. And then maybe we'll start talking about other long-term plans."

He smiles, the dimples on his cheeks making my heart squeeze like they have since the very first time I laid eyes on Griffin. My husband is totally a DILF. And he's all mine.

"I like the sound of that," he says, standing to join me to the kitchen,

The twins start babbling to each other, giggling and chattering in a way that makes me smile. They're perfect. Griffin's perfect. Well, that's not true. No one is perfect, but they are perfect for *me*. And I can only imagine what the future holds for us.

"Me too," I say, grinning at my gorgeous husband.

I'm so, *so* blessed.

PENTHOUSE PRINCE

Lexington Dane was my brother's best friend growing up.

We did everything together.

He taught me how to throw a punch, how to change a tire...and he taught me how to kiss. I fell hard and fast, and gave him all my firsts.

I promised I'd wait for him...

But I'm done waiting, because he went off to college and never came back. He took his fancy business degree and moved to New York City, where he promptly became a real estate mogul— turning every penthouse and apartment project he touched into gold.

It's been ten years, and now he's back and needs a favor...someone to watch his little girl. That's right, the cocky penthouse prince and heart-breaker extraordinaire Lexington is back with an adorable two-year-old daughter. Guess who he wants to watch her?

I've never been able to say no to him. I might agree to be the nanny for his precious little angel, but there's no way in hell I'm falling for her hot-as-sin daddy.

Acknowledgments

Thank you so very much to my wonderful readers! You make all of this possible, and even though some days are stressful, I don't take a single minute of that for granted. A giant bear hug to all the book bloggers who so graciously provide support and visibility for my books. Thank you!

I'm so grateful to my amazing team . . . you guys are incredible. At the risk of leaving anyone out, I will just say it takes a village, and I'm so glad you are part of mine.

Big squeezes to my husband, John, for the unending support he provides. Thank you for being my loudest cheerleader, my biggest advocate and my most complimentary reader.

Get Two Free books

Sign up for my newsletter and I'll automatically send you two free books.

www.kendallryanbooks.com/newsletter

Follow Kendall

Website

www.kendallryanbooks.com

Facebook

www.facebook.com/kendallryanbooks

Twitter

www.twitter.com/kendallryan1

Instagram

www.instagram.com/kendallryan1

Newsletter

www.kendallryanbooks.com/newsletter

About the Author

A *New York Times*, *Wall Street Journal*, and *USA TODAY* bestselling author of more than two dozen titles, Kendall Ryan has sold over two million books, and her books have been translated into several languages in countries around the world. Her books have also appeared on the *New York Times* and *USA TODAY* bestseller list more than three dozen times. Kendall has been featured in publications such as *USA TODAY*, *Newsweek*, and *In Touch Magazine*. She lives in Texas with her husband and two sons.

To be notified of new releases or sales, join Kendall's private Mailing List.

www.kendallryanbooks.com/newsletter

Get even more of the inside scoop when you join Kendall's private Facebook group, Kendall's Kinky Cuties:

www.facebook.com/groups/kendallskinkycuties

Other Books by Kendall Ryan

Unravel Me

Filthy Beautiful Lies Series

The Room Mate

The Play Mate

The House Mate

The Fix Up

Dirty Little Secret

xo, Zach

Baby Daddy

Love Machine

Flirting with Forever

Dear Jane

Finding Alexei

The Two Week Arrangement

Seven Nights of Sin

Playing for Keeps

All the Way

Trying to Score

Crossing the Line

The Bedroom Experiment

Down and Dirty

Crossing the Line

Taking His Shot

How to Date a Younger Man

Penthouse Prince

For a complete list of Kendall's books, visit:
www.kendallryanbooks.com/all-books/

CPSIA information can be obtained
at www.ICGtesting.com
Printed in the USA
LVHW011749110820
662922LV00010B/998

9 781733 672993